•A QUINNIE BOYD MYSTERY•

a SIDE of SaBotage

C. M. SURRISI

Carolrhoda Books • Minneapolis

Carolrhoda Books
A division of Lerner Publishing Group, Inc.
241 First Avenue North
Minneapolis, MN 55401 USA

For reading levels and more information, look up this title at www.lernerbooks.com.

Jacket illustration by Julie McLaughlin.
Map design by Ingrid Sundberg.
Backgrounds interior: © Gordan/Bigstock.com.

Main body text set in Bembo Std 12.5/17. Typeface provided by Monotype.

Library of Congress Cataloging-in-Publication Data

Names: Surrisi, Cynthia, author.
Title: A side of sabotage : a Quinnie Boyd mystery / C.M. Surrisi.
Description: Minneapolis : Carolrhoda Books, [2018] | Summary: "A fancy fine dining establishment has opened in Quinnie Boyd's Maine town, creating new competition for her father's humble café. When things start to go wrong at the café, Quinnie suspects the people behind the new restaurant are to blame" —Provided by publisher.
Identifiers: LCCN 2017006437 (print) | LCCN 2017033440 (ebook) | ISBN 9781512498523 (eb pdf) | ISBN 9781512448368 (lb : alk. paper)
Subjects: | CYAC: Mystery and detective stories. | Diners (Restaurants)—Fiction. | Sabotage—Fiction. | Friendship—Fiction. | Maine—Fiction.
Classification: LCC PZ7.1.S88 (ebook) | LCC PZ7.1.S88 Sid 2018 (print) | DDC [Fic]—dc23

LC record available at https://lccn.loc.gov/2017006437

Manufactured in the United States of America
1-42555-26211-10/12/2017

For Chuck, who would happily eat a
Gusty burger every day

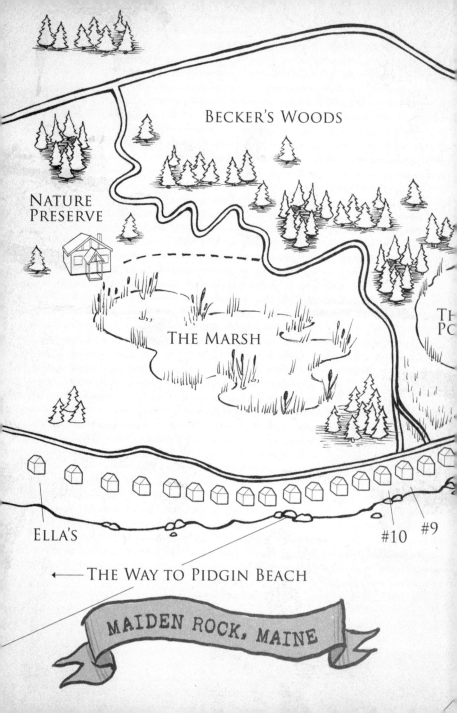

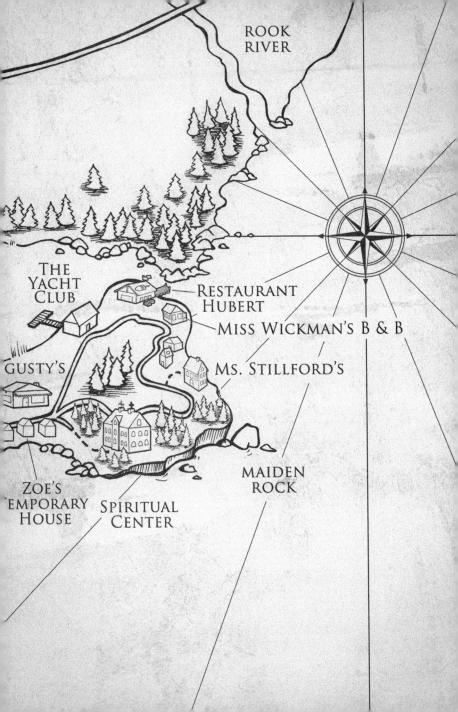

ROOK
RIVER

THE
YACHT
CLUB

RESTAURANT
HUBERT

MISS WICKMAN'S B & B

GUSTY'S

MS. STILLFORD'S

ZOE'S
TEMPORARY
HOUSE

SPIRITUAL
CENTER

MAIDEN
ROCK

I

I sidestep a patch of creeping beach grass as I walk down Mile Stretch Road. Green crabs catch my eye, scurrying over nearby rocks. Beyond them, gulls stop shredding a piece of seaweed long enough to squawk at me and my friends for interrupting their meal.

We all have to share this place. The crabs. The gulls. Me, Quinnette Boyd. Ben Denby, scientist-jock. Ella Philpotts, New York transplant and exotic painted bird. Dominic Moldarto, cap-wearing sci-fi expert and all-around nice guy. And Maiden Rock's summer tourists, back in town for June.

Ninth grade in Rook River is over as of yesterday. I survived. After all those years of being tutored in Maiden Rock, way out here on the rocky coast of Maine, I was more than a little nervous going to a big school outside of town every day. Having Ella, Ben, and Dominic around made it easier. And now my best friend from birth, Zoe, is coming home.

But Dominic is leaving.

I take a deep breath of salty air and let the late-morning sun warm my face. I feel the gravelly sand beneath my flip-flops. Why can't I pick and choose what happens? And how it happens? Why, why, why? I ask you.

Ben jogs ahead of us, then doubles back, burning off energy. "I really need to run today," he says.

Ella throws her arm around my neck and touches heads with me. "Q, you need to try my newest nail color, Blissful Blue Azure."

I laugh. This girl. She's turned me into a sparkly-toenail-polish wearer just like her. And—*woo hoo!*—when Zoe comes home tonight, my two best friends will finally meet. I've been telling them about each other for more than a year, and soon they'll be in the same place. Sure, they're about as different as chocolate pudding and lemon pie. Ella is a questioner, like me. A digger-into-problems. And yes, this gets us into some tricky situations. Zoe, on the other hand, is super cautious. When we were eight, she wouldn't even help me crawl across the beam in Ms. Stillford's carriage house so I could dangle from a rope like a trapeze artist. I mean, seriously!

Still, the thought of them meeting gives me goose bumps of excitement.

And Dominic is leaving in thirty days, which has me tossing and turning at night wondering if I will ever see him again. He is—and I don't say this out loud very often—my boyfriend. We're copacetic (one of Dominic's favorite words). So a tiny voice in the back of my head keeps telling me that, if he's leaving, I need to start protecting my heart. But I'm not going to think about that today.

And oh, there's this: my dearest darling teacher, Ms. Stillford, who tutored me for my first eight years of school, has been bored out of her gourd since retiring last year. Now she's taking her husband, crusty lobsterman Owen Loney, on a big see-America trip. And since you can't run a lobster pound while you're seeing America, he sold his lobster pound and put his trawler up for sale. But following the sale, he's been a mopey, coffee-drinking fixture at the end of Gusty's café counter, which I can see upsets Ms. Stillford.

It's piling on. I'm like, *enough stress already.*

"Hey, look!" Ella points to the café, where Dad and Owen Loney are wrestling a ladder through the back door.

Ben takes off running toward them. "'Chuppta?" He's always ready to get involved in a project, especially one that might involve climbing on a roof. "Need help?"

Dad and Owen Loney exchange raised eyebrows as if to say, *Do we look like two old guys who can't set up a ladder?*

"Thanks, Ben," Dad tells him. "I think we got it."

"What are you doing?" Ella asks.

"Measuring how much sign space we've got," Dad says. "For Quinnie's mom."

He makes it sound like he's humoring Mom. But there's a good reason he and Owen Loney are headed for the roof.

This is the craziest change of all: The guy who bought Loney's Lobster Pound is this chef from Boston with a famous temper. He's turned the place into a super-fancy restaurant—named after him. *Restaurant Hubert* has only been open a month, since the middle of May, but it's the first real competition my dad's café has ever had. A gourmet restaurant reviewer called it "coastal agri-modernism." I think that's supposed to be high praise.

Mom may be the Maiden Rock sheriff, the real estate broker, the postmaster, and the mayor— all of whom want the town to boom—but like me, she doesn't want the café to suffer because of some restaurant up the street serving singed-carrot vinaigrette and raw-beet foam. Gusty's is the heart of this little coastal village and a Maiden Rock institution. Still, the place could use some publicity. We've all been trying to convince Dad of that.

After Restaurant Hubert opened, I made T-shirts that say: *Gusty's Café—Home of the Gusty Burger and Lobster Fries.* Mom has been lobbying for a new sign. Clooney Wickham, the all-in-one cook, summer server, and assistant manager, wants Dad to plant flower boxes in the front. Even Ben's uncle, John Denby, the director of the local nature center, thinks "patchin' up the pah-kin' lot might be a good thing." We're all on edge about this Hubert place.

But not Dad. He isn't afraid of what he calls an "uptight place with hefty prices." He belly-laughed when he heard Hubert's signature dish would be "lobster quenelle poached in seaweed broth and finished with a beam of light."

"What respectable Mainah will pay for that?" he said. "Me, I'm sticking with burgers and fries."

I'm not so sure. Some people like fussy food once in a while. I might even want to try some of it. Like maybe the subzero chocolate pudding on a red bamboo stick. But Dad says he's not buying a three-thousand-dollar anti-griddle just to make a fudge pop.

We stand there watching Dad and Owen Loney snap a tape measure across the current sign (which probably went up when Dad was my age), proving how easily entertained we are here in Maiden Rock. I hear a car coming and turn to see a sunny yellow truck heading for Circle Lane. The writing on the door says *Randy's Organic Free Range Poultry*. It's stopping at Restaurant Hubert, no doubt. The egg-yolk yellow of the truck almost hurts my eyes.

Across the road, a line of beach houses is getting some summertime repairs. A man in overalls scrapes peeling paint off the Morgans' house, getting it ready for a fresh layer of white. A crew of workers is washing the windows at the Chathams' place. (It takes a lot of rubbing to clean off a winter's worth of caked-on sea salt.) And opposite Gusty's, John Denby is fixing the railing on the front steps of the Lambert house.

I get a small heart-quake when I think that in a few short hours, Zoe, her mom, and her dad will be piling into that house. I imagine hugging Zoe, introducing her to Ella, introducing Ella to Zoe . . . then, *friend perfection.*

"Perfection?" Ella says.

"What?"

"You said, 'Perfection.'"

Great. I'm talking out loud and don't even know it. "Perfection: my two best friends are going to meet each other soon."

Ella nods. She's been listening to me go on about this for a while. I know she's not as thrilled about it as I am. I get that. That's because she doesn't know Zoe yet. But she will.

I gesture to the house across the street. "It's going to be weird having Zoe live there." The Buttermans will be staying in the Lambert house until Dominic's family leaves. Dominic's family rented the Buttermans' house while his biology professor parents spent their sabbatical year at Rook River College. Ella and her dad lived there for a stretch before that. And soon Dominic's room, which had also been Ella's room, will turn back into Zoe's room, the room where she and I had so many sleepovers.

"Too bad Dominic's parents didn't buy a house here in Maiden Rock," Ella says.

We both turn to look at Dominic. Shorts, a T-shirt with a sigma sign on it, Vans with black socks, and that hat. I saw that hat for the first time a year ago. Squat like a golf cap, and plaid. This one's actually Son of Hat, as he calls it, since Hat was lost at sea during the great vampire caper. I look down at my chest, at the pi sign on my own T-shirt, the one he gave me last August, after a summer of figuring each other out.

"He's turned me into a geek," I say.

"A totally cool geek," Ella says. She leans into me and smiles. "Wait, is that an oxymoron?"

Ella and I look at Ben, who is elbowing Dominic and making comments about the origin of the tape measure while Dominic listens with rapt interest. Who would have guessed that these two would bro-bond like this? When they met a year ago, tempers flared. Ben: *You can't prove that vampires exist.* Dominic: *You can't prove they don't.* Ben: *Grr.* Dominic: *Grr.* Now here they are, tight as can be.

Maiden Rock is like that. It brings people together.

I look at Ella, then think about Zoe, only a few hours away.

I can't wait.

2

Inside the café, Mom and Ms. Stillford are seated at a central table, looking at Mom's not very artful drawing of a new sign for Gusty's.

Ben and Dominic head over to our regular spot, while Ella and I stop to look at Mom's idea.

"It's a good start," Ms. Stillford says. I recognize her diplomatic voice.

Mom holds up the drawing admiringly. "I like it. It says *Maiden Rock*."

"What are those?" Ella asks as she points to some red spots in the corners.

Mom looks at the blobs like she doesn't understand the question. "Lobsters," she says. "Two on each side." Ella and I don't say anything. Mom continues, "You know, for Maine . . . lobsters . . . like in Gusty's famous lobster fries."

"What do you think?" Ms. Stillford asks me.

I don't want to criticize Mom's drawing too much, since I agree that Gusty's should have a new sign. "Maybe we should—er—hire a designer."

"Okay." Mom drains her cup of coffee and rolls up the drawing. "I see that my efforts are not going to cut it." She laughs. "I'll take this to Rook River and have it done by a professional. We're going to have a lot of traffic in town this summer, and we want Gusty's to snag as much of it as we can." She gives me a quick hug and heads outside to talk to Dad.

"You kids coming over this afternoon?" Ms. Stillford asks me. "That carriage house is calling your names. I so appreciate that you're doing this for me."

"We're ready," I say. Believe it or not, I truly can't wait to clean out her carriage house and run a tag sale for her. "But Zoe is coming home this afternoon, so maybe we could wait for her and do it tomorrow?"

"Of course! That would be wonderful. I can't wait to hear all about her time in Scotland." Ms. Stillford smiles at me with twinkling eyes. "You must be so excited, Quinnie."

I feel like Ella has tuned out our conversation. I elbow her and say, "I am. I can't wait for Ella to meet her."

Ella smiles. Not a big excited smile. Just a little one. I understand. She doesn't know what to expect. But I can't help myself. I'm a silly mess, waiting for the three of us to be together. It's been two years since Zoe left. Well, one year and eight months, technically, but it seems like an eternity.

"So, I'll see you tomorrow?" Ms. Stillford asks.

"Absolutely," I say, and then head for where the guys are seated.

A thin man wearing a black T-shirt and jeans comes in, walks to the counter, and starts to survey the café like he's a dog looking for a bug on the wall. Up, down, and across. He squints to read some of the raggedy titles on the lending library shelf. *Hauntings in Ancient Maine Mansions, Atlas of the Maine Coast, Narragansett, Arundel, Blueberries for Sal*, and dozens of old *Yankee Peddler* and *Down East* magazines.

Clooney Wickham wipes the counter in front of the man and hands him a menu.

"Coffee?" she asks.

"Herbal tea?" he replies.

"Lipton," she says.

"No herbal?" he asks.

"Nope. No herbal."

"Water will do, then."

As she walks away, he adds, "Bottled—if you have it."

When Clooney returns with the man's bottle of Poland Spring, he says, without looking at the menu, "I'll take a kale salad."

Clooney stands there with her hands on her hips. Ella and I turn to each other with raised eyebrows.

He presses on. "With a citrus vinaigrette."

Clooney shakes her head and sighs. "House dressing on mixed greens with tomato. Or, we have coleslaw."

The man looks at her as if he's assessing how far he can push this line of questioning.

"What's in the house dressing?"

I cringe. From my seat, I can see the man's profile. His hair is dark blond, slick and shiny, neat and tight. He has a strong profile with a large nose and chiseled cheekbones. He looks a little like a skinny male model. A skinny male model is asking the fearsome Clooney Wickham to recite the ingredients of the house salad dressing. I would not want to be him.

Clooney takes an annoyed breath, then rattles off: "Olive oil, red wine vinegar, orange juice, lemon juice, honey, orange rind, onion, salt, celery seed, paprika, dry mustard, sugar, and a partridge in a pear tree. And no, we don't grow the celery ourselves."

He leans back. "I guess that'll do."

Clooney takes the menu from him. This guy has Restaurant Hubert written all over him. What's he doing here? I make a mental note to tell Dad how patient his normally snarky employee was, how she didn't *do a Clooney* on this guy when she easily could have. At the same time, she just told him how Dad makes his greatest salad dressing ever, so I'm a little uneasy.

Ella leans toward me and whispers, "What do you think? One of the cooks at Restaurant Hubert?"

"Probably." We both know it's not Hubert himself. Everyone in town has heard the big boss has a shiny bald head.

"I bet your dad's dressing would be great on a kale salad. Do you think he'd try that?"

"I don't know, maybe. As long as he didn't have to spray it with sea mist and serve it on a deboned dolphin fin."

We laugh so hard at the thought of this that the rest of the café looks our way.

"Anyway"—I pull myself together—"Dad

wouldn't charge twenty-five dollars for it. I heard a salad at Restaurant Hubert costs that much."

Before Ella can comment on the going rate for a kale salad back in New York City, Dad walks back in and Dominic calls out, "I've got a menu idea for you, Mr. Boyd."

"Oh, yeah?" Dad rolls his eyes. "Whatcha got this time?" Dad's getting used to people around town recommending Maiden Rock versions of foodie dishes.

Dominic slips a paper from his pocket and reads: "Gusty burgers sous vide."

This stops Dad in his tracks and causes him to give up a big belly laugh.

"What's *sous vide*?" Ella asks.

Ben volunteers, "Dom and I have been studying up on this stuff. It's where you vacuum seal the burger in a bag and cook it submerged in water at low heat—"

"That's a good one, guys," says Dad. "But I don't think I'll be boiling my burgers in a bag. I'm sticking with the griddle."

The slick-haired man at the counter grunts. Although he has the house salad to occupy him, he's obviously been listening to all of this. And he practically does a double take when Sisters Rosie and Ethel bustle through the main door and head for the counter. The sisters used to live at the Our Lady of the Tides Convent. Nowadays, and after a sketchy episode a while ago involving a convent fundraiser and the disappearance of Ms. Stillford, they're running a cat rescue in an old lighthouse on Pidgin Beach, south of here. But they still come to Gusty's every day for a meal or a piece of pie.

The stranger turns and cuts the sisters a look like they're annoying him. He pushes some lettuce around the plate with his fork, then spears a piece and looks at it like it's a scientific specimen. Finally, he puts it in his mouth.

I can tell Dad's studying this guy as he chews. It doesn't take long before the deliciousness of the salad registers on the stranger's tongue. He takes a second bite, then a quick third. He pulls a piece of paper and pen out of his pocket and starts writing.

"Will you be wantin' anything else?" Clooney asks the man, having fielded the sisters' pie order. "Blueberry pie? Whoopie pie? Cinnamon bun—"

"What did you say was in this dressing?" he asks her with his pen poised.

Clooney looks at the pen and paper in his hands and backs up against a stack of coffee cups, which clink against each other in response.

Dad steps in. "So glad you like it. It's a Gusty's trade secret."

I immediately think, *Good for you, Dad!* He's starting to feel a little protective of his recipes. Anyway, why does this stranger want to know? Our salad's not exactly Hubert's style.

Dad sticks his hand out. "I'm Gusty. This is my place."

The guy opens his mouth and says something, but I miss it because Owen Loney leans over our table and asks me, "Who's that?"

"We think he's from Restaurant Hubert," I answer.

"Fool place," Owen responds.

Sister Rosie's a critic too. "I read in the paper about the beam of light. I don't get it."

Owen Loney adds, "That's an insult to a decent lobstah." He grumbles as he watches the slick-haired man stride out of the café.

"You know," Ella says, "if you really want to give Gusty's a face-lift, we could repaint the benches out front," says Ella.

"That's a good one. I'll do that," Owen Loney says.

"We could make some flyers with coupons for specials and put them in the mailboxes," I say. "And put new ones out every week."

Ella adds, "We could do a Facebook page, Instagram, and a Twitter handle."

"And Snapchat," Ben says, pulling out his phone. "It would be like ten seconds of me eating lobster fries."

Dad arrives at our table in time to hear our ideas. "Don't worry, you guys. It's just a healthy rivalry."

"Yeah, I don't know about that," I say.

Ben offers, "We could fix up the dock behind the café, and boats could sail right across the pool."

Dad looks back toward the kitchen, in the direction of the tidal pool. "We'd only be sailable at high tide. We found that out years ago. Mucky mess at low tide."

"Let us do *something*, Dad," I say. "Coupons?"

"I don't make more money by giving away food that everybody around here already loves. And don't get me started on Facebooking, tweeting, and snapping."

Ben can't help himself. "Snapchatting."

"Flower boxes?" I say, sounding a little desperate.

"Clooney's on that," Dad says. "Look, you relax for a bit, have some fun, or better yet, go help your mom with welcome packets for the summer people. We'll talk about the rest later."

"Please, Dad," I say, getting more worked up about it. "This is really happening. That guy was from Restaurant Hubert, I know it. He was trying to steal your dressing recipe. At least get some kale or something."

3

Now that we've put off cleaning Ms. Stillford's carriage house until tomorrow and Dad won't give us anything to do around the café, Ella, Ben, Dominic, and I have around five hours until Zoe arrives, so I guess we're forced to go to the beach. Dad's right. We should relax and have some fun.

I've walked and run and played on this beach my whole life. I know every rock and crevice and crab on it. The big outcropping to the north shelters a channel that flows into the Maiden Rock Tidal Pool, where I learned to sail. The cliff above the towering white ex-convent building—now a spiritual center—is where "sailors were lured by sirens' calls, and scorned maidens threw themselves to their death," or so the Maiden Rock historical marker says.

Dominic and Ben run full-out down the beach,

kicking up sand, a blur against a fuzzy blue and white background.

Ella's in sharp focus next to me. The sun bounces off the plastic jewels of her flip-flops, turning the sea foam pink and yellow for a second. We walk in the surf until bites from the fifty-five degree water turn our skin red.

I raise my voice over the soundtrack of crashing surf and cawing gulls. "Are you excited?"

She smiles. "Sure. But I'm not exactly in the zone you're in."

"Fine. It's true. I'm in outer space."

"All I know about her is what you've told me." She rolls her hands in an *on and on* motion. "You know, what you guys did when you were three and four and five and six and seven and eight—"

"Okay, shut up. I get it."

"And let's not forget all the photo albums with Halloween costumes, and when you each lost your first teeth, sailing lessons, beach bonfires, sleepovers—"

"*Stop!*" I put my hands over my ears and run laughing toward the guys. "I know. I'm sorry!"

Ella races after me and grabs me around the waist. "Just kidding. You know I'm going to love her." She pulls back. "Wait. She has her front teeth now, right?"

I try to push her into the ocean. She tries to pull

me down. We wind up sitting on a big rock.

"I haven't been that obnoxious, have I?"

She scoops some water and splashes it at me. "No. I'm messing with you. Mostly, you just go on about her after you've talked to her on the phone. And that's only like every other month."

"That's funny. Mostly, I'm telling her about you on those calls."

Dominic runs up to me and drapes a wet stinky seaweed necklace around my shoulders.

"Eew!" I duck and push it on to Ella, who tosses it over to Ben. He takes it and flings it out to sea.

"It'll be back," Dominic says as he climbs onto a rock next to me.

Ben plops down on the beach below us. "I wonder what it was like in Scotland."

Dominic replies, "Scottish."

"She was on a farm, right?" Ella asks, as if I haven't told her about it a hundred times before.

"A four-hundred-year-old sheep farm," Ben answers.

I explain again: "Her dad is a researcher. He studies sheep parasites."

"I suppose somebody has to," Ella says.

I search her tone for a hint of meanness but don't hear it. She's just being her New York quipster self.

"The farm didn't even have Internet or decent reception," Ben says. "My uncle couldn't call them, except on a landline."

"Zoe said that was superexpensive, too," I say. "That's why I could only talk to her every other month."

"For like two hours!" Dominic says.

"Not that long!" I punch him.

"Dumbo's a talker," Ben says.

"Ben!" Ella looks shocked.

"What?" Ben says. "Back in the day, that's what we always called Zoe. She has big ears."

I look at Ella, and she's got this horrified expression on her face. "I am *not* going to call her that."

I try to roll Ben over into the sand. "You are so stupid, Ben Denby," I tell him, even if I'm cracking up a little.

We've completely slipped into our old ways, like when he and Zoe and I used to goof around, call each other names, build forts in the sand, and play pranks on the summer kids. It's total eight-year-old behavior, but we can't stop ourselves. As predicted, the seaweed rope washes back ashore, so I grab it and try to tie Ben's feet.

"Big Foot." I point at him.

"Swampy." He points at me.

"I get the Big Foot," Ella says, looking at Ben's giant running shoes. "But *Swampy*?"

"Aw, Swampy, that's cute." Dominic crinkle-smiles, and his dimples show.

"The first year we took sailing lessons, Quinnie swamped the boat three times," Ben says.

Of course, this causes me to grab Ben around the neck and start in on a noogie while he tackles me around the back of my knees.

I fall to the sand, panting and laughing. Ben tries to tame his hair, which is now sticking up in every direction. Something about it reminds me of that old ache of a crush I used to have on Ben—that is, until two years ago, when Ella moved here and he went bonkers for her, and a year later, when Dominic moved here and I fell in heartthrob with him.

Life used to be so simple when it was just Ben and Zoe and me. In my twelve-year-old mind, I was going to grow up and marry him. But now I'm not thinking about marrying anybody. I'm just thinking about how important Dominic and his geeky, hat-wearing, sci-fi loving playfulness have become to me. And he has soft cheeks too, even though whiskers are starting to grow there every which way. And I love the shape of his shoulders. And he's smart. And kind.

And funny . . . but I'm not going to think about that right now.

My phone buzzes with a text, and I jump.

"Oh, no."

"What?" asks Dominic.

"Mom says the Buttermans are hung up in customs. They won't be here until late."

"How late?" Ben asks.

"*Late* late."

Dominic stands up and stretches. "Well, Swampy, want me to walk you home?"

I stare at him like, *I can't believe you said that*, and his face turns pink. I'm about to say, "Shut up, Hat Boy," but it doesn't sound clever enough.

Ben says to Dominic, "Want to help me clean the sailboat?"

Dominic turns to me and says, "The offer still stands."

"Go, go," I say. "You guys better have the cleanest sailboat in Maine by tomorrow morning."

"Come on, Swampy, *I'll* walk you home," says Ella.

"Not you too!" I say. "Keep this up, and we'll find nicknames for you both."

"Hey, look!" Ella points out to sea.

I stop and focus on the horizon. It's Owen Loney's fishing trawler.

"Isn't that the *Blythe Spirit*?" Ella asks. "I thought he sold it."

"I think it's still for sale at a marina in Rook River," I tell her.

We stand there and watch the boat motor along the coast. It comes closer to the breakwater and slows. Owen Loney, wearing his signature cap, gives us a single wave.

"What's he doing?" Ella asks.

"I think he's having a hard time parting with it," I say.

Ella frowns. I look at her standing in the sand with her Garnet Shimmer Red nail polish and bejeweled flip-flops. "I think we should call you Glamazon."

"I can work with that, but I'm not going to let you get stuck with Swampy. We'll have to find you a new nickname."

"And one for Dominic."

"And I have no idea what Zoe will be like, but there is no way I'm calling her Dumbo."

"But Ben can stay Big Foot," I say.

"With those bear paws? For sure."

4

I wake up to a brilliant yellow-white sun popping up over the Atlantic and blasting through my bedroom window. In that split second between being asleep and awake, I forget that Zoe might be only a few houses away. It all rushes back to me in one deep breath, and I bolt out of bed. The clock says five seventeen as I run down the hall to the bathroom and brush my teeth. From behind Mom and Dad's bedroom door, I hear Mom's voice.

"Quinnie. Don't go to see the Buttermans before nine."

I sneak back toward my room.

"Quinnie? Tell me you heard that. Not before nine."

Grrr. "Fine," I say, then throw on jeans and my pi shirt.

I'm downstairs in the kitchen by five thirty, making toast. When Dad comes in, I jump.

"Morning, Quinnie," he says.

"Morning, Dad."

He drops a pod in the coffee machine and presses extra-large. Of course he would be up by now. He has to start the cinnamon buns at the café.

"You heard your mother, right?"

I can barely taste my toast, because food is the last thing on my mind. "Nine o'clock is like the middle of the day."

"No need for hyperbole, Quinnie. They got in very late. They'll have jet lag. Let them be for a bit."

I sink into a chair at the kitchen table. The maturity that's been forming so nicely inside me is threatening to give way.

Dad sits down and peers at me over his coffee cup. "Why don't you come to the café with me and hang out until it's a decent hour to go see Zoe?"

I consider this. Gusty's has the benefit of closer proximity to the Buttermans' temporary residence. I'm pretty sure that once I'm there, Dad'll give in and let me go earlier. He's a softie that way.

"Come on." He pats my arm. "Get your shoes, and let's go."

The drive up Mile Stretch Road is eerily quiet, except for the twenty-four-hour soundscape of breaking waves. When we reach the parking lot, old Buster the seagull and his flock rise up in excitement. The opening of Gusty's means the beginning of a day of leftover french fries being tossed to the neighborhood scavengers.

"Hang on, boys and girls. It'll be a few hours," Dad tells them. He unlocks the front door and flips on the lights. "See, Quinnie, you're not the only one waiting for something this morning." I look at the house across the street. All the windows are dark.

Dad starts passing through the kitchen, and I hear the great suction sound of the refrigerator door opening. Next comes the sound of Dad placing a large saucepan on the stove, and *bloof*—lighting the gas flame.

By the time all the chairs are down and tucked under their tables, I can smell the sweet, spicy, buttery goodness that Dad is spreading over rolled-out sheets of creamy white dough. Next, he starts dumping ingredients for blueberry muffin batter into the mixer.

It's now six thirty. I check the house across the street for signs of life. Still dark. A pickup drives up to the café, and its engine goes quiet. Owen Loney gets out, adjusts his cap, and shuffles inside. The café doesn't actually open until seven, but Owen's allowed in any time he wants. He still dresses as if he's just come in from a lobster-trap run. Poor guy.

"Mornin', Quinnie," he says. "You're up early. I wonder why!"

Just as I'm bemoaning that everyone in town knows my business, Clooney Wickham comes in to start her day.

"Whoa, Quinnie! You watchin' for Zoe to wake up over there?"

There is nothing to do but pitch in and help Clooney fill the sugar bowls and salt and pepper shakers and fold the napkins. She has to supervise my napkin folding. Her special contribution to a more competitive Gusty's is a new paper-napkin design.

By seven thirty, the buns are coming out of the oven, the espresso maker is steaming out shots, Ms. Stillford has joined Owen Loney, and Sisters Rosie and Ethel have arrived at their favorite table.

"Sit with us, Quinnie," Sister Rosie says as she licks frosting from a bun. "I can't believe how early we have to get here these days to grab a cinnamon bun. They just fly right out the door."

Sister Ethel sips a double espresso and looks to the ceiling like she's experiencing Heaven. "That's a fact. Gusty's has never been so busy."

I don't know what they're talking about—I count only seven people in the café, including me, Dad, and Clooney. Then I realize it's a sort of pep talk, or one of those things you hope will come true if you say it enough times.

By eight, my leg's jiggling against the leg of the chair, annoying everyone. It's still quiet across the street, although three more people have entered the café. A text pings on my phone.

Ella: *Where are you?*

Me: *Gusty's.*

Ella: *I'll be right there.*

By eight thirty, she arrives and orders a coffee to go. I interrupt Dad as he's taking blueberry pies out of the oven. "Can I leave now? The whole town is awake."

He nods. If you didn't know my dad, you would think he was just nodding to keep me from distracting him while he handles four-hundred-degree lumps of bubbling sugar, but he doesn't miss a thing. That nod was accompanied by a wink.

Once Ella and I cross the road, my instinct is to reach for the doorknob and walk in. After all, the Buttermans are like family. But—it's not actually the Buttermans' house, and it's been one year and eight months since I saw any of them, and frankly, the situation intimidates me a teeny bit.

I knock.

Nothing.

I knock again—a couple times.

Someone stirs inside. A slow, plodding movement follows—Dominic would call it a zombie walk.

Mrs. Butterman opens the door slowly, standing in her robe with her hand above her eyes, squinting into the morning light. She doesn't say anything at first; she just backs up and lets us in. Then she hugs me tight and waves hello at Ella and points upstairs. "First door on the right."

I realize that I've never been in this house before. An obstacle course of crates, boxes, and suitcases fills the hallway, and the stairs aren't where I expect them to be. Still, I take the steps two at a time, beckoning Ella to follow me. At the first door on the right, I don't even knock. I burst in. I'm sure Zoe's as awake as I am and as eager to see me as I am her.

Inside the dim room, there's a lump under the covers and a head with coppery red hair on the pillow. She'd mentioned a different color, but whoa.

The body under the covers stirs.

I say, "Zoe?"

She rolls over and opens one eye. "Q!" she says in a sleepy voice, then throws back the covers.

It's her, all right. No mistaking those blue eyes. But her face is longer and thinner, and for sure she has a hair revolution going on. I want to scream and hug her, but it's a different her. So I hesitate.

"Oh my gosh, you haven't changed a bit," she says, stepping over her open suitcases to hug me.

I don't know what to say. She looks so different—so much taller. Do I look this changed? I guess not.

I lean back, and all that comes out of my mouth is, "You weren't kidding about your hair."

She fluffs it and says, "Yeah, what do you think?"

I hesitate. It's involuntary.

Her face falls. "You don't like it."

"No, I'm just surprised, that's all. It's nice. It's cute."

She rolls her eyes. "Quinnie Boyd, you're a terrific faker." Then she sees Ella. "Hi, Ella."

"Hey," Ella says back with a small wave of her hand. She's wearing her favorite eye shadow, Precious Pale Penuche, with a matching eyeliner.

Compared to the two of them, I look like a pilgrim.

Zoe starts picking through her exploded suitcases and pulling out souvenirs and telling us about them. She's brought home rocks, plaids scarves, books, statues, flags, bags of candy, sheepskin pelts, and more. Ella drifts to the window, which overlooks Gusty's front door.

"Ms. Stillford and Owen Loney are leaving the café," she says, pointing down at the parking lot.

I almost forgot my promise to Ms. Stillford. "Zoe, come on, get dressed! We're cleaning out Ms. Stillford's carriage house."

As Zoe scrounges around for something to wear, I join Ella at the window. The café's parking lot is about two-thirds full. That's light for the peak of breakfast time. Even though the road is busy, not many cars are turning into the lot. A minivan, topped with luggage, is obviously just arriving in town. Then there's the Miller family's car, headed out of town. And at least two unfamiliar vehicles slow down, then drive past Gusty's in the direction of Restaurant Hubert.

5

Zoe bops down the stairs and out the door of her temporary house, and I'm struck by how tall she really is out here in the daylight. It seems like she's grown three inches. I'm five feet, and she has to be at least five-five. She walks between me and Ella, taking our arms and leading us up the road toward Ms. Stillford's.

"I've missed this place," she says, "with its fishy seaweed smells and salty air. So much better than sheep manure."

"I miss the garbage smells and exhaust fumes of Manhattan," Ella replies, "but this does have its charm."

I try to think of what I like about Maiden Rock, but at that moment, I can't come up with anything. I'm too fascinated by Zoe and Ella walking arm in arm, neither of them looking completely comfortable.

When we reach Ms. Stillford's, the guys are carrying boxes out onto the lawn. Zoe sees Ben and waves in a big arc. "Hey, cousin."

Ben stops, stares, leans forward, and stares some more. "Wow! Look at you, Rubylocks."

As Zoe runs to give Ben a hug, Dominic walks out of the carriage house, bouncing a large box on his hip. "Welcome to Ali Baba's treasure chest."

Zoe says, "You must be Dominic."

"That's me," he says. "And you are Zoe."

"Zoe!" Ms. Stillford calls out as she hurries toward us. "Welcome home!"

Zoe spins around, catches sight of Ms. Stillford, and takes off running again. They give each other such a big bear hug that Ms. Stillford's feet come off the ground. The two of them fall into a conversation about the trip home, the sheep farm, and how much has happened while Zoe's been gone.

"Come on, Zoe, you've got to pick your prize for helping me out with the sale," Ms. Stillford says, leading us into the carriage house. A moment later, she reaches into an open box and pulls out what look like magnifying glasses attached to a fold-out stand. "I should probably keep these."

Ben and Dominic exchange glances that say, *Not again!*

This goes on all morning. We take something down, and Ms. Stillford almost always puts it in the stay pile, giving us a story about each item. The stories are fun to hear, and she's sweet as she tells them, but sometimes my mind drifts to the Gusty's parking lot. I wonder how the breakfast business turned out.

By one o'clock, our stomachs are grumbling, and I tell Ms. Stillford that we're going to Gusty's. We walk by way of the old lobster pound—I mean, Restaurant Hubert. It looks like there's quite a lunch rush inside. I sense that I'm glaring at the building when a figure walks from the kitchen door out onto the road. It's the guy who wanted the salad dressing recipe. I've decided to call him Slick. Moving several strides ahead of our group, he doesn't seem to notice us, and we fall silent and start to walk slowly. Even Zoe seems to understand that there's something off about this guy.

He passes the yacht club; we pass the yacht club. He turns and walks down Mile Stretch Road; we turn and walk down Mile Stretch Road. He walks into Gusty's. We all look at each other with surprise.

Slick takes a seat at the counter, while I pull the group toward a table behind him. It's not our regular table, but my intuition tells me I should keep an eye on him.

Dominic leans close and says, "I can see the headline now: *Restaurant Hubert Employee Eats at Gusty's.*"

Clooney hands Slick a menu. "What'll it be today? Still no kale, in case you're wondering."

"I'll have the Gusty burger and fries," he says.

"Lobster fries?"

He leans back. "Lobster fries?"

"Fries with the same kind of dip you get with a lobster."

"Hmm. Sure. I'll try it."

"You'll want the blueberry pie too."

I have to give it to Clooney, she knows how to make Gusty's a complete dining experience.

"Sure," he says.

"And coffee. It's wicked good."

"And coffee. Since it's *wicked good.*"

When Clooney brings the Gusty burger and lobster fries, it happens—just like it always does. The juice runs down the man's arm after he takes his first bite of the burger with mustard and onions on a toasted English muffin. He rolls his eyes and sighs. There's always a sigh after the first bite. Then come the lobster fries. He lifts the little paper dipping cup and smells the orange-colored melted butter and lemon. Next comes the pinky finger in the butter.

A questioning look crosses Slick's face. Then, with fry after fry, he delivers the butter to his mouth.

Before the man's plate is clean, he's trying to weasel the ingredients out of Clooney. What spices are in the burger? In the butter? How does Gusty's achieve the crispiness of the fry?

This time Clooney is on to him. "Nope. Nada. Nein. Ain't telling. Mind ya own business."

Dad appears at the counter and shocks me with his friendliness toward Slick. "Hello, Willy. How's it going today?"

"Just great, Gus. Be even better if your waitress would tell me your secrets," Slick says.

Dad laughs. "No big secrets here. What you see is what you get. Beef, bread, mustard, onion, potatoes, butter, lemon."

"Okay, be that way. It's good. Very good. But you could take it up a notch with wagyu beef, maybe organic Maris Pipers, Vichy onion aspic bites . . . you get the picture." Slick wipes his mouth after scraping up the last bite of blueberry pie.

"Perfectly," says Dad.

Once Slick pays and leaves, Dad comes over to our table. "Do you believe that guy?"

"What are *Vichy onion aspic bites*?" I ask him.

"The best way to describe it is onion Jell-O."

"Gross," we all say at once.

"You called him Willy. Willy who?" I ask.

"Willy Lovelace. Lead line cook at Restaurant Hubert."

"I think he's trying to steal your recipes, Dad."

Dad shakes his head. "If he is, he isn't going to get them. But really, there's room enough for both of us in Maiden Rock. What's most important is not the type of food you serve, it's your passion for the food. Hubert Pivot has one kind of passion. I have another."

I look at Dad and think, *Poor Dad, you are so naive*, but—because he has such a sweet smile on his face—I can't bring myself to say it.

6

Back at the carriage house, Zoe starts to get to know Dominic, who can talk to anyone and be super funny on the spot. Ben plays strongman, lifting chairs and old dressers. Ella gets caught up in an old leather-bound copy of *The Wonderful Wizard of Oz*. Halfway through it she says, "I'm not going to let her get rid of this." I find a box with handmade dolls wrapped carefully in muslin. In an instant, Zoe and I are seven again, sitting in Ms. Stillford's dining room, cutting swatches of fabric and making small dresses for our prize possessions. Mine is Eleanor; hers is Marianne.

And now they're in an old box, dresses not entirely finished. Why? I guess because we moved on to something else. I wonder if Eleanor should be the one thing I take from the carriage house.

That night, we scatter. Dominic has to go somewhere with his parents. Ella and her dad have some company passing though from New York. Ben goes running. Zoe has to unpack. I sit in her room and watch her, but I'm too preoccupied to actually help. I have the café and Hubert Pivot's line cook on my mind.

"That Slick guy is trying hard to suss out my dad's recipes."

"What would he do with them? Restaurant Hubert wouldn't use them, would it?"

"Maybe he wants them for his own restaurant someday."

"That's a compliment, Q."

"That's stealing."

* * *

Willy Lovelace's creepy behavior is still on my mind when I wake up the next day. I decide Mom should know about it.

When I walk downstairs, she's sitting at her desk, wearing her sheriff's uniform, browsing the news online. She's on the edge of her chair, leaning on her elbows, chewing on her thumbnail.

"Morning, Mom."

"Morning, Quinnie," she mumbles.

"What are you reading?"

"Reviews of Restaurant Hubert."

I sit on the arm of her chair and try to read over her shoulder. "What does this one say?"

"'Hubert Pivot has struck haute cuisine gold with his new Restaurant Hubert, in the faraway ocean-side hamlet of Maiden Rock, Maine. With only fourteen tables, this farm- and sea-to-table establishment provides an intimate dining experience. The menu selections exhibit thorough knowledge of and dedication to multisensory cooking, validating the hefty prices, though the officious flair with which rock-star chef Pivot approaches his dishes—wafting smoke across the surface of the restaurant's marbled tea eggs in a seaweed nest or finishing the lobster quenelle with a beam of sunlight—is somewhat comical. Nonetheless, Hubert is accomplishing what he has set out to do, making Restaurant Hubert a destination for connoisseurs of culinary ingenuity.'"

"Is that a good review?" I ask.

Mom scrunches her face up. "I think it means that the food is excellent, if that's the kind of food you want and you can afford it."

"Have you seen the guy with the slick hair that works there?"

"Yep. Willy something? Dad mentioned him."

"Did he tell you Willy is trying to get Gusty's recipes?"

"Dad told me the guy asked, but of course your father's not giving them to him." She swivels in her chair, forcing me to stand up. "Hold on—this better not be what I think it is. Quinnie, Gusty's recipes are safe. Don't make a mystery out of this."

"Don't you think it's weird? The snooping?"

"I think it's annoying as all get out, but the guy's not getting them. And you can't stop him from trying to guess the ingredients." Mom shuts off her computer. "Besides, they're useless to a fancy restaurant like Hubert's."

I start to walk out of the room, and she calls me back. "We've got a check-in this morning that I need you to do."

"Which house?"

"Rankin's."

"Isn't that one of the big ugly ones?"

Mom laughs. "Stop it. It's not ugly . . . It's . . . garish."

She's not kidding. There are a few houses on our small beach that have been turned into an out-of-stater's idea of Maine, not the real thing. The owners almost never live in them, just rent them out. For huge amounts. Usually, they hire Mom to coordinate things. Mom calls it "throwaway money."

"Who's renting it?" I cringe thinking about some of the annoying people who've summered in these houses.

"Her name is Billingsley."

"Have you met her?"

"No, just emailed with her." Mom pulls out a welcome packet and sets it on her desk, along with the key. "I'll leave this at the café. When she shows up, give her the packet and show her to the house, and make me proud of you. Okay?"

"Where are you going?"

"I've got to go to Rook River for a course on this new body camera. I'll be back by dinnertime." She points at her collar and points at me. Unlike last year, when Mom got a body cam the size of a deck of cards, this one is tiny.

"I know, I know," I say, "you're watching me."

* * *

"Gus," says Sister Rosie, "look at this one. Farm greens with shallots over millet cake, with fennel salad and tomatoes."

"Yep, yep. I see that," says Dad.

I catch his eye, and he winks at me.

Sisters Rosie and Ethel are camped out at their table, finishing cinnamon buns and espressos. Sister Rosie has a pile of photocopied recipes in front of her, and Dad is leaning over to look at them, nodding his head. It's ten o'clock, and the café is about half full. That's pretty good for midmorning.

"And this one." Sister Rosie pulls out another sheet. "Aged cashew cheese and black sesame-seed paste on rice crispins, with tarragon and apple compote."

"Yep, yep. I see that."

My crew is gathered at the café—with the exception of Zoe, who I guess is still readjusting to Eastern Standard Time. Ben and Dominic are chowing down on Gusty's famous blueberry muffins, served cracked open and oozing with melted butter.

"Your dad is a good sport," Dominic says.

"He should try some of those recipes just so he can compete with Hubert's," says Ella.

"He doesn't think so," I say. Dad's listening to all of Sister Rosie's ideas, but I know he'll take those recipes and file them away where they'll never reach a Gusty's plate.

"Whoa!" Ben leans over to check out a car that has just pulled into Gusty's parking lot. It looks like someone's ride in an old movie. Big bulbous front fenders and googly-eyed headlights.

"Jaguar XJR," Dominic says.

"Love the metallic marine blue," Ella says. "I'd like to have that in a nail color."

We all turn to look at the owner of the blue Jag as she comes through Gusty's door. She's a tall woman wearing white pants, a black sweater, numerous strands of beads, and a faux tiger-skin scarf-hat over one ear. She carries a large vinyl leopard-skin-patterned handbag. Rhinestones adorn her sunglasses; her gloves look like accessories for an old-timey tea party; and then there is her dog. The small white pup is wearing a one-piece outfit that's supposed to look like cowboy attire: blue jeans, a yellow checked shirt, and a cow-skin patterned vest. And a brown hat that looks like it belongs to a mini cattle driver.

Our whole table groans quietly. She has to be Mrs. Billingsley, today's check-in.

Clooney walks up to her and says, "No dogs allowed."

The woman replies, "Ridiculous. Groucho is a certified companion dog. He goes *everywhere* with me."

"Certified by who?" Clooney asks.

"He's a companion dog, and that's all you're allowed to ask. Now, where am I?" It's unclear whether she means the building, the town, or the state.

Dominic shocks me by getting up and walking over to her and saying, "Gusty's Café, Maiden Rock, Maine."

"I need to check in to my beach house."

I speak up. "I'll get your welcome packet."

Dad comes out of the kitchen with a plate of blueberry muffins, just in time. "Welcome to Maiden Rock. My daughter, Quinnie, will show you the way to your rental." He gives me a look that reminds me Mom tells him *everything*.

The woman checks me out as if I'm suffering from an appalling lack of patent leather. "Well, let's go." Her big handbag catches in the door as she walks out.

"I'll go with you," Dominic says to me.

"Thanks. I'll be right out." I duck behind the counter to grab the welcome packet while Dad, who's standing nearby, tells Clooney the rules for service dogs. I'm starting to listen in when Dad turns and says, "Quinnie, Mrs. Billingsley's waiting." Fine. Nobody told me about a dog. But if nobody cares, then nobody cares.

7

In the parking lot, Mrs. Billingsley has decided to let Groucho do his business near one of the flower planters. Dominic walks around the blue Jaguar, leaning over periodically to inspect it more closely. When Groucho is finished, he darts over to Dominic and puts his little cowboy paws up on Dominic's leg. Mrs. Billingsley walks away from the poop pile, checking something on her phone.

I say, "Ma'am, you have to clean that up."

Mrs. Billingsley either doesn't hear me or pretends not to.

I say it louder. "Ma'am, you have to clean up after your dog."

Mrs. Billingsley looks up as if in a phone-daze and says to me, "It's small, he's small. It'll dry up and blow away in no time." She opens her driver's-side door. "Now, which way are we going?"

Dominic says to me, "I'll ride with her to her rental."

"Fine," I say. "I'll walk down and meet you there."

Dominic starts to get in the Jag, but Mrs. Billingsley shakes her head. "Just give me the address. I'll meet you there."

I'm wondering how this is all going to filter back to Mom . . . and I can't believe I'm picking up the poop.

Dominic waits for me while I bag and toss the little lumps. While I'm griping about it, a car pulls into the parking lot from the direction of Circle Lane. It stops to let Slick out. I realize the man behind the wheel is Hubert Pivot. I haven't seen him in person, but there is no mistaking him from his picture in the paper. He's as bald as a volleyball, with ears that stick out like wings.

Slick lingers by the open passenger door. They don't seem to notice us standing there. "It wasn't that bad!" he says to his boss. "It said you struck haute cuisine gold."

Hubert grumbles and tightens his grip on the steering wheel and says something about "seventy-one percent bookings."

Slick says, "A lot of people still go to this joint."

I distinctly hear Hubert say, "They won't for long."

49

Before Slick slams the door, he says, "Don't forget the spring onions."

Hubert peels out, and Dominic and I beat it to the rental to do my duty to Mrs. Billingsley, the words *They won't for long* running over and over in my mind.

* * *

Billingsley tells Dominic to carry in her bags, then to watch Groucho, who really is a cute little dog. His owner forces me to walk around the house with her and record everything she notes is wrong, broken, or inadequate. Dominic and I don't leave for another hour.

Once that hour's up, I stop by Mom's office to drop off Mrs. Billingsley's list of complaints, and then Dominic and I head to Ms. Stillford's, where the save pile is growing. I swear that she must have come out overnight and moved half of the sell items over to the save heap.

Dominic's still trying to decide which cool piece of junk he wants. He's leaning toward a View-Master slide viewer and a box of two hundred slides from *National Geographic*. Ella has claimed Ms. Stillford's vampire costume, complete with fangs and a wig. Zoe wants her Marianne doll. And Ben wants the full thirty-three volume set of *Encyclopedia Britannica 1994.*

I'm going through a box of little salt and pepper shakers, all individually wrapped in yellowed news-paper. Ceramic pigs, lambs, snowmen, skaters . . . but I can't focus. *They won't for long*—it's stoking my suspicions. I walk out of the carriage house and call Dad. He answers on the first ring.

"Hi, kiddo. Sup?"

"Are you busy?"

"Not so much. Midafternoon lag."

"Is Slick there?"

"Willy? Nope. He was here for lunch but he's gone."

"Dad, I heard him talking about Gusty's with Hubert, and he said"—I think hard about exactly what he said. I've learned that exaggeration does not help in these situations—"'There are still people eating at Gusty's,' and Hubert said, 'They won't be for long.'"

"Where did you hear this?"

"In the Gusty's parking lot. Hubert was dropping him off."

"Right. Well, I'm not sure what to say other than that's the way competition goes. Everyone would like to have the most customers."

"But Dad, he said 'not for long,' like something was going to happen. Like he was going to *make* something happen."

"Seriously, Quinnie, what can he do? Out-advertise us? Besides, Slick—as you call him—is eating here on a regular basis. *Spending money* here. I wouldn't call that a problem."

I don't think Dad's getting it. "You should ban him from Gusty's. He's trying to steal your recipes and who knows what else."

There's a pause on the other end. I can hear his mind going to that place where I'm an alarmist playing detective again. But he softens his tone. "Your point is so noted."

"Okay, Dad. Think about it."

I go back into the carriage house and announce, "We have to do a publicity campaign for Gusty's. And we have to do it *now*."

* * *

Over the next two days, I take note of the number of people eating at Gusty's. I can't exactly say how big the drop is, but for a time of year when summer homes are full and weekly rentals are always booked, the café's definitely not as crowded as usual. At night,

I hear Mom and Dad talking in the kitchen about gross receipts and net revenues.

My crew has made flyers that say *Gusty's Café— Family Owned Since 1918* and put them in all the local mailboxes, along with coupons for a cinnamon bun, a bowl of chowder, or a piece of blueberry pie. I needed Mom's help to pressure Dad on the coupons. He repeated his argument: "I don't see how giving away food makes any money, especially the food I always run out of." But Mom urged him to try it. He agreed once we added, *with purchase of a sandwich.*

An Instagram account is probably still out of the question. And the friendly fancy food suggestions keep rolling in.

Ms. Stillford brings Dad a recipe for probiotic goat yogurt with *pruneau* puree. She says he could blow a flute over it. Dad smiles and shoves it in a drawer. Ben's uncle, John Denby, hands Dad a scan of his mother's handwritten recipe for *Granny's Bread Ball Soup.* Ben whispers to me that Dad should throw it away, because it's made with beef lard and will give our patrons heart attacks. Dad tells John, "I appreciate the thought." Owen Loney tells Dad that his "ma" used to make "porridge with a butterfat lump in it." Dad says, "You don't say, Owen." Then he whispers to me that people are confusing "old-timey with newfangled."

On the morning after the butterfat lump incident, Dominic and I are sitting at our usual table, designing a new T-shirt that says *Gusty's Café—Best Blueberry Pie in Maine*. Dominic is pressing us to add an infinity symbol when Slick comes in with another man who looks like he's also from Restaurant Hubert.

Dominic points to their feet. "Those are Crocs. They're the preferred footwear in a commercial kitchen."

"How do you know that?" I ask.

"Ben and I saw them wearing those goon shoes before, and we looked it up," he says.

"You guys don't have enough to do."

Dad walks over to Slick's table with two mugs and a pot of coffee.

"Fill 'er up," Slick says.

The other guy nods at his cup like he'll take the same.

Slick opens the plastic-covered menu and points to various items, telling his buddy that he should try this or that or that one too. "It's good stuff," he says.

Dad hears this and puffs up a bit. "Glad to hear you like it."

"You've got some interesting flavor medleys going on here," says Slick.

Dad beams. Then he does the craziest thing he's ever done. He says, "I bet I could even beat Hubert's in a cook-off."

Slick laughs.

Then Dad gets majorly feisty. "Really, you tell Hubert I challenge him to a cook-off."

Slick uses the kind of voice my dad always uses when he's telling me to *simmer down*. "Okay, okay, I'll pass that along to the boss." He looks at his buddy. "What do ya think, Carl? Fresh versus fried."

As Dad walks back toward the kitchen, he underlines his point: "I'm not kidding."

* * *

Later that evening, I'm sitting on our back porch watching the waves, and I get a text from Zoe.

Zoe: *Want to meet on the beach?*

Me: *Sure. I'll text Ella.*

Zoe: *Just us, maybe?*

Me: *K. Meet you halfway.*

Little alarm bells go off in my head. What's this about? Doesn't she like Ella? What if Ella sees us walking without her? Will that hurt her feelings? Am I being stupid? Is this no big deal? Yeah. It's probably no big deal.

I stick my head in the kitchen, where my parents are sitting at the table, assembling welcome packets for summer renters, and I hear Mom say, "You did what?"

Dad says, "I challenged him to a duel."

"Not seriously?" says Mom.

I jump in. "I heard it, Mom. He challenged Hubert to a smackdown."

"Smackdown, taste test, cook-off, a food competition. Call it whatever you want." Dad is swaggering around the kitchen, waving a telephone emergency-contact list. "Bring it on."

"Oh my gosh, Gus!" Mom says.

"I'm meeting Zoe for a walk on the beach," I say. I don't really want to get sucked into this conversation.

Mom and Dad both turn at the same time. "Be back before dark."

As the door closes, I hear Mom say, "Did he agree?"

"I just mentioned it this afternoon."

Cold, wet sand flicks at my ankles. It's almost seven o'clock, and the tide won't be in for a couple hours. Still, the surf hits the rocks hard, spraying the right side of my body with salt water. It feels strange to be walking past Zoe's real house on the way to her rental house. When I look up to her old room, where Dominic currently lives, TV light is bouncing off the walls. He's alone—he could have called me to do something. That hurts a little bit, since he only has three weeks left. Then he walks in front of the window, carrying a box. He's packing. *Pinch my heart. He's really leaving.* But I put this out of my mind.

A tall, thin figure jogs toward me, red hair bouncing wildly in the early evening light. For a second, I ask myself who it is before realizing it's Zoe.

She flips my hood up over my head. I duck, then reach out and pull at her ruby locks.

"You hate the new look, don't you?" she says.

"I do not. I don't hate it." I jam my hands into my pockets and look straight ahead to avoid looking at her massive head of hair.

"Well, you don't love it."

"I'm just getting used to it, that's all. It surprised me. It looked different when I pictured it in my head."

"It's not like a Merida 'do or anything. It's just hair."

This gets me laughing.

She wags her head in my face, and I push it away, laughing harder. "It's . . . so . . . red!"

"It's a little weird, isn't it?" Zoe says.

"What?"

"I don't really feel like I live here anymore."

Her voice is almost pitiful. I don't know why, but it surprises me. I never expected her to not feel at home in Maiden Rock. "You will. Wait until you get back in your house. And I'm here, and Ella's here."

"Q, I don't know Ella." She kicks up some sand, runs in the surf, and yells, "I like her nail polish, though."

I stomp in after her. "And she likes your red hair."

Zoe fails to maintain her enthusiasm. "I miss Scotland already."

8

The next morning, Ella's dad's car motors up the road and rolls to a stop in front of my house. I jump in the back seat and lean forward between them. "Morning."

"Good morning, Quinnie," Mr. Philpotts says. He's not very convincing about its goodness. He has dark circles under his eyes, like he's been up all night writing one of his crime novels. I've learned to recognize "writer face" from seeing it regularly at Ella's house.

"He needs a depth charge," Ella says.

"That's a fact," says her dad.

"Zoe coming?" Ella asks.

"I haven't talked to her since last night. I'm sure she'll show up."

Ella turns to look at me like, *Is something the matter?* I'm hesitant to admit things are not going as perfectly as I'd hoped.

Inside Gusty's, the smells are breathtaking. We've arrived just as the blueberry muffins are coming out of the oven.

Mr. Philpotts waves at Dad and sits down at the counter. Dad immediately turns to the fancy Italian espresso maker he bought last year to satisfy discriminating caffeine drinkers like Mr. Philpotts and Ella's aunt Ceil and uncle Edgar.

When Ella and I slide into our regular seats, she asks, "What happened to you last night?"

Now, I have been known not to tell the whole truth sometimes. But I have never fudged it with Ella, and I'm not going to start now. "I went for a walk with Zoe." I can tell this bruises her feelings.

"On the beach?"

She says it like that puts a paper cut on top of the bruise.

Something tells me that I shouldn't say, *She wanted it to just be the two of us.* So I say what I know is true. "She misses Scotland and doesn't feel at home here anymore."

I must have major disappointment on my face, because Ella pats my arm.

"You know what Monroe Spalding says, don't you?"

Since Monroe Spalding is the detective in her

father's crime novels, I can't imagine what he'd have to say that applies to this situation. "What?"

She tips her head and says, "Always follow your first instinct."

"What does that have to do with Zoe?"

"I have no idea, but think about it."

I'm thinking about it when the door to the café opens and in walks Slick, followed by Hubert himself. This is my closest look yet at his shiny bald head, those big ears—like open car doors—and his white chef's coat, with its collar unsnapped and flapping.

Everyone, I mean everyone, sucks in a breath, and the room falls silent.

Hubert stands in the center of the room, turning his head like he's looking for the person most likely to be Dad.

Dad comes out of the kitchen, wiping his hands on a towel. He and the bald man meet in the center of the café.

Sister Rosie eyes the door like she might make a run for it. People shuffle uncomfortably in their chairs.

Slick walks in between them like a referee about to do a coin toss.

Hubert's neck is blooming red.

Dad's chest is rising and falling.

Slick says to Dad, "Gus, this is Hubert Pivot."

Dad sticks his hand out, friendly-like.

I swear there is a beat of time when we all think Hubert won't go through with the handshake. Then he extends his arm and says, "How do you do? You have a nice place here." His voice is quiet and flat, but at the same time, there's a smirk on his face.

"Thanks," Dad says, and everyone in the café seems to relax. "I haven't seen yours yet."

"Well, stop by sometime. I'll cook something up for you," Hubert says.

I'm hoping Hubert doesn't ask Dad if he likes aspic, because that could send this whole thing into a tumble.

"So, Gus," Slick says, "Hubert wants to take you up on your challenge."

Dad broadens his stance. "Well, excellent."

"How do you want to do it?" Hubert asks, as if he's done it a variety of ways.

Dad looks a little unsure.

Mr. Philpotts, who has been watching along with the rest of us, interjects: "I have a friend who's the editor of the *Rook River Valley Advertiser*. Maybe he'd put his restaurant critic, the Secret Diner, on the case? You guys just run your restaurants, and the Secret Diner will pop in and out—anonymously, of course.

At the end of, say, a couple of weeks, the Secret Diner could announce the winner in the paper."

Dad and Hubert study each other's faces for signs of fear or confidence, then both nod and agree.

Ten minutes later, Mr. Philpotts has made the call.

"It's a go," he says. "The Secret Diner will commence incognito visits in two days. This will go on for seventeen days. And in the end, we'll know whose food passes the test of our local tastemaker."

I want to ask him why seventeen, but Mr. Philpotts goes ahead and explains that the Secret Diner's doing two weeks' worth of stops, plus a few off days, so he can keep the restaurateurs guessing. Dang. This is sounding like a bigger and bigger deal.

Dad and Hubert shake hands one more time before Hubert and Slick leave. Slick orders two whoopie pies to go on his way out.

When the door shuts behind them, applause breaks out in the café. Dad bows from the waist.

Ben and Dominic arrive a minute later.

"Was that who I think it was?" Ben asks.

"It was," I say.

"Hubert in the flesh," says Ella.

"I could take him," says Ben.

"There's going to be a competition with the Rook River paper's Secret Diner as the judge," I tell them.

Dad, meanwhile, is moving from one table to another, laughing and high-fiving people.

I'm not sure how I feel about this. If he wins, that's great. But what if he loses? When I see how happy he is, I hope like crazy this works out.

"Gusty's will grab the W, no sweat," Ben says.

"I'm not sure I get it," Dominic says. "They don't make the same kind of food. At all. How do you compare Gusty's chowder to fiddlehead ferns in custard?"

We look at each other vacantly.

"That's a great question," I say.

* * *

At home that evening, while Dad prepares dinner, Mom is at the kitchen table, making a list of everything that has to be done at Gusty's before the competition starts. A new text makes her phone ping every few minutes.

"Touch up paint, get the new sign up"—*Ping.* She stops to check the text, then continues. "One more task: print new menus—"

"Whoa, whoa, whoa, Margaret." Dad turns around, holding a jar of Dijon mustard in his hand. "What new menus? We don't need new menus."

"Just a reprint and new plastic," she says. "Some of them are sticky."

"Okay, then," Dad says, his hackles going back down. "As long as we're clear. We've had that same Gusty's menu for four generations. Every Gusty has cooked it and cooked it the same way." He spoons some mustard into a small bowl and adds fresh chopped herbs. "It's never failed us."

"I'm not saying the menu isn't perfect." *Ping.* Mom stops to read another text. "But what if we added one dish that is . . . a little forward-thinking?"

Big mistake, Mom. I back away from the splash zone on this.

"Forward-thinking? What, does it have to jump onto the plate and turn into a frozen mist?"

Mom's getting frustrated too. "I don't know, Gus. Maybe one dish that demonstrates you could run a Hubert's kind of restaurant if you wanted to. You've already got comfort food covered, but how about an item that competes head-on with one of his? It would be impressive." She puts her phone on the table. "Everyone in town is suggesting a recipe. Listen to this. These are the texts I'm getting." She taps her phone. "Beet brownies, kale chips, udon noodles in organic chicken-bone broth—"

"Let me think about it. You know, it's not like I don't know about all that haute cuisine business. It's just that people will go to Hubert's once, think it was fun but too expensive, and that will be it."

After dinner, I'm walking upstairs to my room, and Dad stops me. "What do you think, Quinnie? Should I trade comfort for kale dust?"

"I kind of agree with Mom, Dad. What would it hurt to try a Gusty's version of one of his dishes?" I put my hand on his shoulder. "Just don't do the bone broth thing, okay?"

9

The town is abuzz at breakfast the next morning over the *Rook River Valley Advertiser*'s splashy announcement. Starting tomorrow, the Secret Diner will begin stealth visits to Gusty's and Restaurant Hubert. I ask Ms. Stillford if she will mind if we pause the carriage house cleanup to spend a couple days helping Gusty's get ready, and she seems almost relieved.

"I'll tuck it all back behind the doors, and we'll get around to it as soon as all this hoopla is over," she says with a definite twinkle in her eye. "This is the most excitement we've had around here since the vampires came to town."

All day, we bust our butts washing windows, pulling weeds from the cracks in the parking lot asphalt, patching dings on the walls—I even learn what spackle is. And Dominic has polished the

Italian espresso machine so the shine hurts your eyes to look at it.

Six or eight more cars of vacationers arrive throughout the afternoon and stop in at Gusty's. They're one-weekers and two-weekers. And Mrs. Billingsley makes an appearance with Groucho.

"Uh-oh, she's *hee-ere*," I whisper to Ella.

Mrs. Billingsley hustles in, takes over a table for four—which immediately annoys Clooney—and picks up a menu by one corner, like the rest might have jam on it. She's probably right, but Mom is planning to solve that problem by tomorrow.

"Is your chowder creamy or red?" Mrs. Billingsley asks Dad.

Dad looks at her like he'd like to escort her out, but he says, "We serve New England clam chowder with milk and cream. The red stuff is from Manhattan. We also serve a fish head soup. Which would you like?"

"What's the fish in the fish soup?"

Dad looks around and says softly, "Whitefish heads with some added cheeks, leeks, and potatoes."

"I don't see it on the menu."

"It's not on the menu," he says. He taps his pen on the order pad. "It's for local connoisseurs."

"Hmm. I'll have that," she says. "And a side house salad."

Dad's not sure he heard her correctly. "The fish head soup?"

"Yes. The fish head soup, please."

Dad walks into the kitchen scratching his head.

Dominic leaves his station at the espresso machine to consult with me at the end of the counter, where I've been folding paper napkins. His face is solemn. "I feel betrayed."

My mind races through all the things I could have done to make him feel this way. Then he laughs.

"Hey! Don't freak out. It's just that I've been here a year, and you've never told me there's a secret soup for real Maiden Rockers."

Relief floods through me. "I nearly got away with it too," I laugh. "Only a few more weeks and our secret would have been safe from you."

"No, really, I want to taste this stuff."

"Fine. But I don't want you going and telling all of New Jersey about it."

Dominic orders his own bowl of fish head soup, which Clooney takes out to him with a doubting glance. She brings a bowl to Mrs. Billingsley's table with an even more skeptical look on her face.

I can only image what Billingsley thinks about the fish head with its flat eye staring up from the middle of the bowl, but she doesn't flinch. She smells it, runs a spoon through it, and tips a stream of broth back into the bowl. After her first taste of it, she adds some salt, which visibly irritates Dad. Next she scoops a potato cube from deep in the bowl and savors it in her mouth. Then she touches the bowl several times with the palms of her hands.

"Mr. Boyd?" Mrs. Billingsley calls Dad to her table.

"Yes? How do you like the soup?" Dad asks.

"It will do, but you must remember to heat the bowls before you ladle the soup into them. Do you follow what I'm saying?"

Dad hesitates. I think he's trying to keep steam from coming out of his ears.

Dominic swivels in his stool at the counter and calls out to Dad: "Mr. Boyd, this fish head soup is fantastic! But the bowl's a little too hot."

Dad smiles.

Mrs. Billingsley makes a *hmmf* sound.

The next time the café door opens, Mom's favorite type of visitors walk in—a middle-aged couple with *affluent lower New England* written all over them. She's got the sweater set. He's got the cashmere V-neck. They look around approvingly and select a picturesque table near the window.

She takes old *Down East* magazines off the lending library shelf and delights at how tattered and charming they are. Clooney has menus in their hands in a nanosecond, and just as quickly gets the scoop on them, which she passes along to us. His name is Robert Lewis, hers is Helena Lewis, and they aren't staying here in Maiden Rock. They're at a bed-and-breakfast near Scavenger's Bay, and they caught the article in the paper on their way through Rook River. They're very polite, according to Clooney. "They never once complained about the temperature of the plates."

One thing I notice, though, is that Helena Lewis orders too much, and Robert Lewis picks off her plate, and they don't take a doggie bag. I kind of take offense at that.

For her part, Mrs. Billingsley leaves before she finishes her fish head soup. On the way out, she tells Clooney to tell Dad that the salad dressing was a pinch too sweet.

* * *

That evening, Ella, Zoe, Dominic, Ben, and I collapse on my family's back porch. None of our seats could be called comfortable. Mom has been talking about getting new rockers and cushions because the current ones are falling apart, but that's on hold until after our Gusty's refresh effort. But we don't care. We're exhausted.

"I'm covered in paint," says Zoe.

"You paint like a toddler," Ben says. "That's why."

"When is your mom getting the new menus?" Dominic asks me.

"Tomorrow," I say.

"Will there be any new dishes on them?" Ella asks.

"I don't know. Dad's thinking about it. I told him he should do one of his dishes in a Hubert style—to be funny, if nothing else."

Dominic, who has been slumped in a rattan chair, jumps up. "I've got it!"

We all yawn.

Dominic continues, undeterred. "It's the fish head soup. Hear me out: it's unique, regional, kinda weird-looking, and above all, delicious. Gusty could modify it *only slightly*—like, I don't know, stick kale in the fish's mouth, add a small slice of beetroot or something."

He stops and waits for it to sink in. We all clap.

"That's brilliant," I say.

"Damn, Dom," says Ben.

"Excellent," says Ella.

"Crackin'," says Zoe.

We all look at her.

She shrugs. "That means nice."

10

Once my friends clear off of the back porch, I go inside to share Dominic's idea. Dad is brushing his teeth when I find him.

"Dad."

He spits and rinses. "Quinnie."

"Do you have a second?"

"Of course. What's up?"

"In my room?"

He turns his whole body to look at me, like *uh-oh*.

I shut my bedroom door, make him sit on the bed, and clear my throat. *Ahem*. "I'd like to talk with you about one thing." I hold up one finger. "And only one thing. About the menu." And then I say very fast, "AndIwantyoutolistenwithoutinterruptingokay?"

He rolls his eyes, but he smiles. "Okay. Go for it, Quinnie."

"What if you made a small change to your fish head soup and put it on the regular menu?"

"Honey, it's off menu for a reason. You know—the heads."

"I know, but just listen. You said you wouldn't interrupt."

"Fine. Go ahead."

"Let's say, after you put it in the bowl with the head in the center and all, you put some kale leaves in the fish's mouth and some grated beets or other root thing sprinkled around, and then sprayed some salt water across the top." I can see this all going into his brain perfectly. A smile rises on his face. He truly gets it.

"I love it."

"You do?"

"I do. I think people will see the humor in it. Plus, who knows, more people may try it. It tastes really good—it's just a little off-putting at a glance. I'll have your mother push those new menus back a day so we can put this thing front and center."

"I'm so glad you like it."

He stands up, and I give him a big hug. He squeezes me back like tomorrow's going to be a great day.

"Nicely done, Q."

"It was Dominic's idea." I feel so proud of him.

"Good man, that Dominic."

As soon as he leaves my room, I text everyone. We bounce that high-five hand around for a while, until Dominic starts sending out pi and sigma symbols, and then the thread gets totally random. But before I go to bed, that sweet, goofy guy sends me, alone, a key-to-his-heart emoji. Sigh.

* * *

The next morning, Dad's and Mom's voices drift into my room and jog me out of sleep. The sun is up, and there are only a few puffy clouds swishing across the sky. I crack open my door. I can't distinguish what they're saying exactly, but I hear "fish heads" and Mom laughing. They sound so happy.

"Quinnette Boyd!" Dad yells up the stairs.

I run to the landing and see him dressed to leave.

"You and your friends should come by a little later and try out my new and improved fish head soup— *with kale*. It's gonna be a great start to the competition, I think."

I'm feeling so upbeat that I offer to go with Mom while she delivers the morning mail.

We drive up to the post office, which is near Ms. Stillford's house, and Mom grabs the canvas bag plus a couple plastic cartons of junk mail. She sorts the mail by house number for Circle Lane, then for Mile Stretch Road, and off we go. We drive on the wrong side of the road for a quarter of a mile so she can put the mail in each mailbox. I've offered to do it a zillion times, but that would break the rules of the US Postal Service, and Margaret Boyd is a stickler for following official rules.

Because we're on the wrong side of the road, which I guess is a rule you can break if you're following a higher rule, the first mailbox we reach is Ms. Stillford's, which we fill mostly with catalogs and a couple of magazines.

We keep going on Circle Lane, all the way to the Maiden Rock Yacht Club, where Mom stuffs a couple envelopes in the club's box, then to the lobster pound that has become Restaurant Hubert, where Mom has two handfuls of mail to deliver.

She slows her car to look at the decal on some car parked by the restaurant.

"What's that?" I ask her.

She points down the side of the building, to the kitchen door, where a man with a clipboard is talking to Slick. He looks friendly. Slick is laughing.

"State health department," Mom says. "Must be a new inspector. I've never seen him before."

We complete the circle and head down Mile Stretch Road, dropping mail at the local spiritual center and a few more houses until we reach the Gusty's parking lot. There, in front of the door, is the same car we saw outside Restaurant Hubert, and the health inspector's getting out, clipboard and all. I kind of wish we'd arrived in Mom's sheriff's cruiser instead of her ordinary real-estate SUV—seeing this guy at Gusty's makes me feel vulnerable all of a sudden.

We don't step out right away. Instead, Mom and I watch the inspector stroll around Gusty's. He's touching freshly painted spots on the clapboard, looking in windows, tapping gutters, leaning over to scrutinize the foundation.

"What's he doing? That's none of his business." Mom gets on her phone and tells Dad what's up. By the time the inspector walks in, Dad's waiting at the door.

"I'm looking for the owner," the inspector says.

"That would be me," Dad says and sticks out his hand for a shake. "Gusty Boyd."

The man shakes hands with Dad and gives him a business card. "Spot inspection," he says without a trace of pleasantness on his face.

"Okay, where do you want to start?"

"Just show me to the kitchen."

The hair goes up on the back of my neck.

"I'm going to finish the mail," Mom says, while I decide to park myself at Gusty's. From a spot at the counter, I watch as this health inspector guy scours the Gusty's kitchen, pantry, freezers, stove, ovens— you name it, he has his nose in it. All this time, Dad and Clooney are trying to run the café. People are pouring in, asking if the Secret Diner competition has started, and Dad is twisting his neck trying to talk to each of them and watch the inspector at the same time.

"Dad, can I help deliver orders?" I ask him.

"Behind the counter, Quinnie."

His answer makes no sense. I don't think he heard a word I just said, he's so distracted by the inspector making marks on his form.

After about a half an hour, the inspector guy scribbles something on the bottom of a form, unclips it from his clipboard, and hands it over to Dad. I can tell Dad's head is swimming—a lot of things must need changing.

"So, when does all this have to be done?" he asks.

The guy points to the bottom of the form. "Right there. A couple weeks from now, I'll be back to re-inspect. If these items aren't cleared by then, I'll be forced to shut her down."

Dad points to one line. "This—the tension on the door gasket. What's up with that?"

"I put a dollar bill between the door and the unit, and it was too easy to pull it out. The door doesn't close tight enough."

"No inspector has ever done a . . . dollar-bill test," Dad says. "The door closes fine. There's no cold air leak."

"I can't help it if other inspectors don't do their jobs." The guy walks away from Dad and opens the door. "See you in two weeks."

Dad turns and walks toward the kitchen, grumbling and pulling a dollar bill out of his pocket.

* * *

That night, pretty much all our closest friends are gathered at our house. It's a welcome home dinner for the Buttermans.

The adults are all sitting around the dining room table, and the topic has turned to the inspection. My friends and I are sitting on the floor in the living room while Zoe shares Super Soor Fizz Balls and Soor Plooms candies that she brought back from Scotland.

The guys make "yuck" noises until the adults tell us to pipe down.

"It was an ambush," Ms. Stillford says. "And on the first day of the competition, too."

"They don't have to tell you when they're coming," Mom says.

"Still, didn't you say he was here a couple months ago?" Zoe's mom asks.

"It was a different guy," answers Dad. "At least I thought it was only a couple of months ago. Maybe it's been longer."

Mom says, "It's silly stuff like a hairline crack in the plastic grill along the top of the refrigeration unit."

"And that's practically decorative," Dad says. "It's been there for years, and no one's ever written it up before. And this gasket tension business? I tried the guy's dollar-bill test and nearly ripped the dollar trying to pull it out. But that and the rest still have to be fixed." All the delight of his tone this morning is gone.

"I'll help," says Owen Loney. "We'll get it all done tomorrow."

Dad and Owen talk about what time they'll get started, while we stay focused on the candy.

Ben's making fun of it. Ella's not eating it.

Dominic braves another piece, and his face twists into a vicious pucker. I don't want any, and I'm not going to pretend I do. Zoe gets sullen and pouty, but I can't cope with the small stuff right now. I have to concentrate on the café.

II

All morning, while Dad and Owen Loney are tinkering, drilling, and taping like mad, Ella and I poke around in Zoe's suitcases, look at her books, listen to her stories—some of which are kind of cool—and try on her tartan skirts, which she says no Scottish people wear in real life. This is my part-way apology for rejecting the candy last night, but I'm still distracted. I drift to the window and watch the traffic across the street at Gusty's.

Mrs. Billingsley and Groucho come and go. The Lewises enter and leave. And a new man arrives. He doesn't look like someone from the Restaurant Hubert kitchen, but he's not dressed like a typical summer tourist either. He looks sort of normal, like a guy who sells pain medicine on TV. I wouldn't be paying him much attention, except he sits in his car a while before he gets out, and then stands in the middle of the parking lot and takes a picture of Gusty's with his phone. That's weird . . . Did I just see the Secret Diner?

At about one o'clock, I see Ben and Dominic jogging down the road from the yacht club toward the café. They spent the morning sailing, so I'm sure they're ravenous. At the same time, Mom pulls up in her sheriff's cruiser and hurries in with a box. I yelp. "The new menus!"

We drop all things Scottish and run across the street.

Once Mom has the menus spread out on a table, the five of us kids crowd around. After searching for the description, I read it aloud: "'Gusty's original mélange of whitefish heads and cheeks. Yukon potatoes, leeks, parsnips, kale, and tomato poached in a rich golden-clam-and-smoky-paprika-infused broth. Kissed with sea brine and served with a fish head in each bowl. A true Maiden Rock experience. Flatlanders be warned.'"

"Dad!" I call across the room. "You did it!"

Dominic yells out to Dad, in his best version of a British accent: "My good man, I would like to try this new item on the Gusty's menu. It sounds brilliant!"

Dad walks proudly toward our table.

"Can we try it?" I ask him.

"Indeed. How many orders?"

I look around the group. No one else raises their hands.

"Two."

I look at the rest of my friends in disappointment. Ella, I understand. But even Ben's chickening out!

Other people in the restaurant are turning their old menus over, scanning them for the item that I just read aloud. We were going to wait until dinner to debut the new menus with customers, but Clooney takes the initiative and starts passing them out.

Five minutes later, Dad is parading through the restaurant with steaming bowls of Gusty's Fish Head Soup, now with fish heads standing up in the bowls like they're about to leap out. Dad's placed bouquets of brilliantly green curly-leafed kale in their mouths.

Dominic leans over his bowl and wafts the aroma into his nose, stretches his arm as a wind up, and dives in with his soup spoon.

"It's even better than before!" he says with a sly smile on his face.

I look at the flat-eyed fish staring up at me from my bowl. He's saying to me, *This is a heckuva thing.* And I sort of see his point. It's a little undignified. I hope people get what's funny about Dad's description and don't think he's trying to be something he's not.

Then the soup's aroma reaches my nose. It's rich and hearty and smells like home—with a twist. "It's fantastic," I say. Yes, this is just right. It's fair play, and it's funny.

"What's this?" Dominic asks. He's holding up a crispy white disk with holes poked in it, which came as a side with the soup.

"Aren't you from civilization?" Zoe asks, rolling her eyes. "Those are pilot crackers. You eat them with chowders and soups and stuff. I might have been away for a while, but you never forget those."

Dominic takes a bite—or tries to. Pilot crackers are notoriously hard because they used to be sea rations. He finally snaps a bit off.

"Soak it in your fish head soup," I tell him.

People at other tables are flagging down Dad and asking if he takes reservations for dinner.

* * *

The five of us hang together into the evening, when we walk along the beach, watching various summer people explore the outcroppings and guessing where they're from: Massachusetts, Pennsylvania, New

Hampshire, the moon. Or at least everyone else is guessing. I can't help thinking about the inspector's car at Hubert's and how he was standing in the doorway, talking to Slick and laughing.

That's what's bothering me, I think. He was *laughing*. With *Slick*. Then when he came to Gusty's, he was all business. And those violations? So many, so minor, so stupid. Laughing with Slick. All business with Dad.

I consider who I'm with before I say this out loud. If Mom or Dad were here, I might hold my thoughts, but Ella, Ben, and Dominic—they're my frontline investigative team. Zoe might have some catching up to do, but we'll cross that bridge when we come to it.

"I think there might be a link between Slick and the stupid violations that inspector found."

"What?" Zoe says. "What are you talking about?"

"I saw the inspector at Hubert's kitchen door right before he came to Gusty's. He and Slick were laughing and joking around."

"And the link would be . . . ?"

Ella answers for me. "The link would be that somehow Slick put the inspector onto Gusty's having some problems. Slick's there all the time and he'd know what to look for. Or maybe he asked the inspector to *think up* some problems."

"To mess up Gusty's the same day the Secret Diner thing is starting," says Ben.

"Exactly," I say.

"Maybe Slick bribed him to do it," says Dominic.

"OMG!" I say. "I bet he did—or Hubert did. Dominic, remember when we were standing in the parking lot and Hubert dropped Slick off? They were talking about all the people eating at Gusty's, and Hubert said, 'They won't for long.'"

"Oh, yeah!" Dominic says. "But if the inspector's crooked—how could we prove that?"

I concentrate really hard on this and come up with a brilliant idea. "I suppose one of us could get a job bussing tables at Hubert's and gather evidence."

"Well, it could hardly be you, Quinnette *Boyd*," Ben says, kicking up some sand at me. "And it can't be me. I'd break all the dishes."

"My dad would never let me," says Ella.

Dominic says, "We're not old enough anyway. I'm fifteen. Quinnie's fourteen. Ella's fourteen. Ben's fifteen. How old are you, Zoe?"

"I'm fourteen, but I wouldn't want to do that anyway. It would be like spying."

"No, Zoe," Ella says. "It would be like investigating."

I have no idea what time it is when the phone rings the next morning. I do know that it's still dark. Next thing I hear, Dad's loudly putting on his shoes, saying a quick good-bye to Mom, and slamming the front door behind him. I wait to see if Mom will come to my room and tell me to wake up, but she doesn't, so I get out of bed and go downstairs.

I find Mom in her office.

"Did something happen?" I ask her.

"*Oh* yes." She is scrolling down a dense-looking webpage about commercial dishwashers and copying down numbers. "That was Clooney. She got to the café to start the baking and found the dishwasher had flooded. The entire load she put in last night is still unwashed, *and* the floor is covered in soapy water." Mom massages her eyes with her fingertips. "So, that little something happened."

"What are you doing?" I ask.

"I'm locating a service rep for the dishwasher."

"Should I go help Dad?"

She turns to me, and for a second, I think she might cry. "Yes—thank you, honey. Go help your dad."

I text Dominic to meet me, then bang on his door on the way.

"What happened?" he asks as he flies out.

"The dishwasher broke, the floor's covered in soapy water, and we have no clean dishes."

Together, we run to the back side of the café. Light spills out of the open kitchen door, and we hear the sounds of a vacuum cleaner and clattering dishes. I pause at the doorway and look in. "Dad, what are you doing?"

"It's a water vac, Quinnie. Sucks up the water," he says.

It looks more like he's swishing suds from one side of the room to the other. "What should *we* do?"

"Help Clooney so she can start baking." We hesitate to wade into the swirls, but Dad says, "Go, go. It's just soapy water."

Clooney is up to her elbows in a steaming sink. She gives us a *thank goodness* smile and peels off her big rubber gloves. "Here you go, kids." She points to the counter, where another pair of gloves lies limp. "And here's the thermometer. Keep the water in the second sink at one hundred eighty degrees to be sure the dishes are clean, clean, clean. But don't put your hands in there. Use the tongs. Dry with these fresh towels."

We pull on the gloves and get to work while Clooney starts the cinnamon buns, blueberry muffins, and pies. A minute later, Ben and his uncle John drive up.

Soon we're all toiling at our assigned duties, including John Denby, who's lying on the floor with tools and a printout of the dishwasher's maintenance manual, trying to figure out what's broken. About forty-five minutes into the task, a truck pulls into the parking lot and noses up to the café's front window. Dad rushes out to meet the repairperson who has sped out on this crazy service call in the wee hours of the morning.

"Hiya," the repair guy says. "Got yourselves a little excitement, eh?"

By this time, Dad has sucked up most of the water. The repairperson asks a lot of questions about our brand of detergent, and Clooney calls out that she's been using the same blue box for years with no problem. About twenty minutes later, the machine's back together. The repair guy says he can't find anything wrong, but we should stick to the blue box. Dad doesn't say anything, but I can tell he thinks Clooney may have used the red box next to it by mistake.

Dominic and I load all the dishes we just washed and dried by hand back into the dishwasher—better safe than sorry, especially now—while Clooney arranges the chairs and tables for the day's customers. By 7:00 a.m., the first one is walking through the door, and it happens to be the man who came alone yesterday, the one who snapped a picture.

Gusty's is ready to take his order.

12

For two days after the dishwasher crisis, everything at Gusty's works like it's supposed to. But my suspicions are growing. Is it a coincidence that we were flooded with suds right after the odd inspection violations? Is it a coincidence that the inspector visited the day the Secret Diner competition was starting? I don't think so. But what proof is there? I keep working on that part of the equation in the back of my mind.

Gusty's is reasonably full at every meal, and my friends and I try to identify Secret Diner candidates. The man who took a picture of Gusty's has been spotted eating there several times and driving past the café toward Hubert's at other times. I check him over again. Not on vacation. No chitchat. He orders all the classics. Sometimes he looks at the food on his fork. He's my number one choice for Secret Diner.

I know he's Clooney's pick. She gives him the royal treatment—the Maine version, anyway, which isn't exactly the finest kind of royal treatment. I've dubbed him Lone Man.

The fish head soup is a hit. Although not everyone gets the humor in it, Ms. Stillford and Zoe's parents laugh out loud when they see it on the menu. The Lewises put their heads together, point to it, and chuckle. But the joke is lost on Mrs. Billingsley, who complains that it's decent soup but Dad should "get that weed out of the fish's mouth. And the bowl still needs to be heated."

I've insisted on hanging around the café—no better way to monitor things—but I'm starting to think my buddies would like to do something else.

"Just for a few hours, Quinnie," Zoe says. "Please. This is making me a little bonkers."

"We could go sailing," says Ben.

"I don't know," Dominic says. "It looked pretty choppy out there."

"I could show you guys how to do some Scottish dances," says Zoe.

Ben grabs his throat and chokes himself.

Dominic says, in his best Scottish brogue, "I dunnuh think so."

Ella looks the other way.

I tell Zoe, "Maybe some time when there's not so much going on. Maybe after the Secret Diner thing, okay?" I hold my breath to see if she dives into a funk, but she seems to shake it off. I think she knew the Scottish dances were a long shot.

"We could watch a movie at my house, except my dad is writing and he really likes it quiet," says Ella.

"No offense, E, but I need to move," Ben says. "Zoe, want to come running with me?"

"I need fresh air too," says Dominic.

I decide to meet everyone halfway. "What about a walk up to Hubert's and back?" I'm thinking of it mostly as a reconnaissance trip, but a walk would at least give everyone some fresh air.

It's quiet for a few seconds.

"I'll go with you," Ella says.

"Me too," says Dominic.

"I'll run circles around you as I'm going by," says Ben.

"I'll just see you guys later," Zoe says.

Great. I guess her feelings are hurt because no one wants to Scottish jig or whatever. But really, that's a little much to ask.

* * *

By the time Ella, Dominic, and I get to Restaurant Hubert, we're deep into a conversation about Slick and Hubert and their possible relationship with the inspector. Could Slick have broken into Gusty's to sabotage the dishwasher, and if so, how? There was no evidence of a break-in. As we approach the restaurant, it looks quiet. There are only a couple cars in Hubert's lot. We walk past the place, all the way to the historical marker on the point. We sit on the bench and watch the surf crash and swirl as we construct various conspiracy theories. I don't really know how long we've been there when Mom calls my phone.

"Where are you?"

"On a walk with Ella and Dominic. We're at the point."

"Something's wrong with the refrigeration unit. Your dad needs a hand. Can you head over and help him out?"

* * *

I walk through the back door of Gusty's at the heart of lunchtime. Dad is frantically shifting meat into ice chests. Clooney is slapping the lids on and handing the chests to Owen Loney, who brushes past us to carry them to his pickup.

"What happened?" I ask Dad, but he doesn't answer due to the fact that he's sticking a thermometer into the meat packages. "Can I help?"

Clooney calls to me. "Quinnie, can you get these orders out? Except table six—I'll do that one."

At table six sits Lone Man, of course. I leave him to Clooney, but that still gives me plenty to do. The dining room is almost full.

I won't lie, I love this. I've wanted to be a server at Gusty's forever, but Dad has said I have to wait until I'm fifteen. But this refrigerator emergency is giving me my chance. I roll up my sleeves and start checking the tickets against the plates coming up.

It's a whirlwind. Dad, Clooney, and I are slipping and swaying around each other as I rush out orders of Gusty burgers and lobster fries, clam chowder, fish head soup, lobster rolls, crab cakes, fried oyster sliders, BLTs, grilled cheese, garlicky coleslaw, pickle-pea salads, brown-sugar baked-bean slices, blueberry pie, and whoopie pies. *Phew.*

The problem is the whirlwind doesn't last. On a normal day at the start of the summer season, the lunch rush would last from eleven forty-five to one o'clock. Now it's twelve forty-five, and Clooney is at the cash register checking the last few people out.

What's even more frightening is that a whole blueberry pie is still in the case. Usually Dad has to bake fresh for the afternoon because he sells out at lunch. Maybe the fish head soup isn't working.

By one fifteen, another repairperson is in the kitchen, this time a guy examining the walk-in cooling unit.

I try to ask what happened, but the conversation is too intense. All I can do is listen.

The repair guy is asking what the temp was when Dad noticed it.

Dad says, "I walked in the cooler at about eleven this morning and I could tell immediately that it wasn't quite cool enough. I looked at the thermostat, and it said forty-five. We never let it get higher than thirty-eight. That's when I called. I transferred all the meat to nearby refrigeration at the proper temps, but I'm worried the cooler's gone on the fritz or the compressor's out or something."

"Do you lock this door?" the repairperson asks and points to the small tumbler lock on the base of the unit, to the right of the refrigeration door.

"No," Dad says. "No need to. Only two of us come in there. Why?"

The repair guy separates the curtain of plastic strips that dangle in front of the open door and motions for Dad to follow. "Well, the temp gauge is in here, you know."

"Yes."

"Who sets it?"

"I do," says Dad.

"So, you set it at forty-five."

"No. I set it at thirty-eight."

"I don't know then, because the compressor is fine. It's cooling to the same temp you see on the temp gauge."

Dad leans around the door and checks out the temp gauge, and yells, "Clooney!"

Clooney hustles to the scene. "Ayuh?"

I can tell Dad is trying to moderate his tone. "Did you by any chance raise the temp in the cooler?"

"Sure didn't," she says with a little surprise in her voice.

"Well, it's set for forty-five, and I set it for thirty-eight."

"Still didn't," she says.

The repair guy senses the tension rising. "Really anybody could have bumped into this in here, knocked a shoulder into it. Maybe that's what happened."

Dad shakes his head. "Yeah, maybe. Thanks." He fiddles with the gauge and then walks out of the cooler and closes the door. "Let's get this thing cooling back down. Any charge for the call?"

"That's alright, Gus," the repair guy says. "I didn't have to fix anything."

"Can I give you lunch? On the house?"

"How about a lobster roll and whoopie pie to go?"

"Done."

Dad looks to Clooney, and she tells the man, "I'll get it for you." As she turns away, she looks over her shoulder at Dad. "Didn't use the wrong soap in the dishwasher, either."

13

It's pitch black outside, and I can't fall asleep. Clouds blanket the sky, blocking the moonbeams that would otherwise shine on the ocean. I lie in bed with my window open and listen to the pounding of the surf and smell the briny breeze.

Something is wrong in Maiden Rock, and my gut knows it. And if I don't figure it out, Dad and Clooney are going to be pulling each other's hair out. This past afternoon was proof of that.

Not to mention, Zoe's wonderful homecoming has been a fizzle. She's in the middle of a big mope-fest, and she and Ella don't seem to be hitting it off either.

Plus, I'm not making the most of every minute with Dominic like I should be. And whose fault is that? Mine. I should be walking on the beach with him before he goes and getting in those last few hours of handholding. But instead, I'm seeing him while we're investigating. Still—that's more important, isn't it?

I know my friends think I hang around the café too much, but I'm starting to believe that I'm not there enough. The decline in lunch business makes me worry. And all the so-called mishaps going on are just too much of a coincidence. Gusty's Café is at risk, which means my family is at risk.

I take a deep breath and apply my well-developed deductive skills. The kinds of things that have happened at Gusty's don't happen by themselves. I have a pretty good idea who's doing them: Slick and Hubert, maybe with the help of the inspector. They have motive: to win the contest. They have opportunity: when the café is closed (or open, in the case of the inspector). The trick is to find some proof.

I want to tell Mom my theory, but before I do, I want to think it through as best I can. Sheriffs hate unfounded speculation. Especially from their daughters.

I think through the little details:

Hubert said that Gusty's wouldn't be popular for long.

Slick was laughing with the inspector, and the same day, the inspector wrote up the café for all kinds of small things that had passed inspection before.

The dishwasher overflowed because someone put the wrong soap in it—and I'm pretty sure that someone wasn't Clooney.

The refrigerator was set too warm because someone turned up the temperature—and I'm pretty sure that someone wasn't Dad or Clooney either.

The time on my phone says 1:30 a.m. I look out my side window, across to Dominic's room. It's dark. Still, I take a chance and text him.

Me: *Hey?*

Dominic: *Hey. Sup?*

Me: *You're awake.*

Dominic: *No. I'm doing this in my sleep.*

Me: *I'm obsessing.*

Dominic: *Meet you down on the beach stairs?*

Me: *On the way.*

It only takes me a minute to throw on jeans, a hoodie, and some Top-Siders, and then I'm sneaking down the stairs, stepping on the spots that I know from experience don't creak. Thankfully, the kitchen door doesn't make its usual yawning sound. Across the way, Dominic's dark figure slips out of his kitchen door, and I catch his hand at the top of the wooden steps that lead to the beach. We park ourselves at the bottom of the stairs like we have so many times in the last year, despite some pretty severe restrictions

(*DO NOT GO OUT AT NIGHT* and especially *DO NOT GO ON THE BEACH AT NIGHT*). But we've been careful, and we haven't been attacked by coyotes or had our blood drained by vampires or anything.

It's our special thing—sitting on this piece of plank, with the smell of sea grass, marine life, and wet sand as our atmosphere. We huddle together.

Dominic says, "Okay, we know all the reasons they might be our saboteurs. What do we say when your mom gives a bunch of reasons they might *not* be? What will *she* say?"

"Good question. She'd say, 'If they were going to mess up Gusty's, why not really cripple it? Why fool around with dinky stuff?'"

"And if they think Gusty's is such a threat, why would they start a restaurant in the same town?" he adds.

"Why would they be so worried when they're getting great reviews?" I say.

"And why would they consider burgers and fries competition?" Dominic pauses. "I don't know. Your mom's hypothetically making a lot of sense right now."

"I know. But still." I drum my fingers on my thigh. "This stuff didn't really start happening until the Secret Diner competition. *That's* why I come back to Hubert and Slick. Even if they don't want to permanently drive Gusty's out of business, maybe they're afraid of the publicity if this big new fancy restaurant loses to a tiny old café."

"It could just be Slick thinking he's helping Hubert, with Hubert not knowing anything about it."

"Well, whether it's one of them or both of them, I've got to stop them." I don't hear the determination I'm listening for in my voice—it's a quiver.

Dominic leans in close to me, squeezes my hand, and says, "And I'm going to help you."

"Aww."

"But we're gonna have to bust them in the next sixteen days."

I push him—just a little bit. "You had to remind me, didn't you?"

We sit there for a long quiet time. Then I say, "I'm worried about Zoe."

"Yeah, she's kind of a mess," he says.

"What should we do about her?"

"We?"

I clasp my hands in front of him. "Please?"

"I am not dancing in a kilt."

"Fine."

We get up and climb the stairs. The grasses sway in the night breeze, and the sound and smell of the ocean haven't changed. Even while something bad is happening, ordinary life keeps going on.

"So are you going to tell your mom what you think?" he asks.

"I don't know yet."

We hug our own special awkward hug. I get that feeling that I should be getting ready to not hold hands anymore.

Okay, fine. What can I say? There may also have been a soft kiss.

It's so sweet my heart hurts. Will I ever have this feeling again? I cry a little bit on the way into the house. Sixteen days. But I push the thought away for now.

* * *

Throughout the rest of the night, I think about ways to approach Mom about this. Casual but with concern. I can already hear her saying, *Quinnie, please don't do this again. You can't go around accusing people of outrageous things.* And I have to admit, I've made some pretty wild accusations in the past, but I've also helped uncover some pretty big crimes.

When I walk downstairs, I can't talk to Mom right away. She's in her office, on the phone, and I realize the family's back in crisis mode.

"It was out when he arrived at five a.m.," she's saying, probably to someone at the power company. "Our auxiliary generator had automatically started up, but we need someone to get the main power back on." Her voice sounds strained. "We use the ovens heavily for the morning baking."

I slip in and wait for her to hang up, but she starts texting as soon as she ends the call.

"Mom?"

"Just a second, Quinnie. Let me tell Dad when the power company will be there."

I take a seat in the office guest chair and wait. When she plops her cell on the desk and leans back with a sigh, I ask, "What's going on?"

"The power was out when Clooney and Dad arrived this morning."

"But it's okay? The emergency generator's on?"

"Yes. It's okay. But I don't know." She gets up, stretches, and walks to the kitchen. I follow her to the coffee. "It's one thing after another."

"Mom." I wasn't quite ready to raise the subject with her, but she has practically raised it herself. "Can I talk to you about something?"

She recognizes the I-smell-a-mystery tone in my voice. "Oh, please, Quinnie. Not now, okay?"

"But Mom. These things that are going on at the café . . . I think maybe they aren't accidents."

"What do you mean, exactly?"

She puts her hands around her coffee mug as if it will give her the patience to hear this through.

I plow through my theory without taking a breath, so she can't interrupt. "It all started around the time Dad challenged Hubert to the competition. I heard Slick tell Hubert that Gusty's had a lot of customers, and Hubert said, 'Not for long.' And then the inspector that we saw talking to Slick came to Gusty's and cracked down so unfairly, and the dishwasher soap was switched, and someone turned the temp in the cooler up, and now the power is out." I take a deep breath.

Mom's tapping her fingers on her mug as she listens. I can tell she's itemizing the reasons why I'm on the wrong trail. After a few seconds, she says, "What was the part about Hubert saying 'Not for long'?"

I explain exactly what I heard when they were in the car. She nods her head. "He could have meant—"

"I know, he could have meant his business was

going to get better. But when you think about every-thing that's happened since then . . ."

"I don't see any connection between Restaurant Hubert and the inspector pestering Gusty's," she says.

"What if Slick bribed him?"

"There's absolutely no proof of that."

"The dishwasher?" I ask.

"Quinnie, there are two large containers of dish soap at Gusty's. One is for the sink and one is for the dishwasher. The one for the sink can't be used in the dishwasher because it makes too many suds. But they're next to each other . . ." She raises her hands like it's obvious that Clooney made the mistake.

"Don't blame Clooney, Mom. She didn't do it. Maybe Slick snuck in and did it. *And* messed with the temperature."

"How could he get inside? We haven't been broken into."

"But Mom—"

"Quinnie, I appreciate your concern, and I feel protective of the café too. But please. *Do not* go around accusing Willy of sabotaging Gusty's. And it would help if you stopped calling him Slick." She gets up and puts the mug in the sink. "These are all easily explainable things."

"The power outage?"

"Your dad says he's needed to update the wiring for a while."

Her phone rings out her favorite song, and she pulls it back out of her pocket.

"Great. Okay," she says to whoever's on the other side of the line.

"What?" I ask after she hangs up.

"The dairy delivery is late."

"I want you to know, Mom, that I'm going to keep my eyes open. This is our family business. This is us."

She looks up at me and catches the quivering of my lip. In an instant, she's hugging me. "I know, Quinnie. There's a lot going on. The contest, and Dominic leaving, and Zoe being out of sorts . . ."

I lean back to look her in the eye. "You know about that?"

"Of course, honey. I talked to her mother. She'll re-acclimate."

"That makes her sound like a zoo animal."

"No. No. Of course not. We all love her. Zoe just needs time. And it's okay to worry about Gusty's. Just please, please don't go overboard. Okay? Promise? No accusations. No calling Hubert, Willy, and the inspector crooks."

I nod my head *yes*. Still, there's something in me that won't let me ignore my instincts. I won't go around accusing Willy and Hubert and the inspector, like Mom ordered, but I can't just look away.

Ella, Dominic, and Ben understand this. I hope Zoe will too.

14

We're gathered in Dominic's room, since his parents are gone for the day. It's littered with boxes, the bed's unmade, the closet door is gaping open, and electronics equipment clutters his desk.

"OMG, my room," says Ella.

"OMG, *my* room," says Zoe.

"Dude, there's like nowhere to sit in here," says Ben.

"We're moving, you weirdos," Dominic replies. "This is what moving looks like."

It looks sad to me. I almost relish the chance to go through the case against Restaurant Hubert instead of dwelling on how Dominic's leaving. "Okay, here's the deal. We're stepping up our investigation of Hubert Pivot."

"Excellent," Ben says, rubbing his hands together. "What's the plan?"

I explain: "We are going to break into Hubert's kitchen tonight and poke around. See what we can find that points to him sabotaging Gusty's."

"Are you sure it's sabotage?" Zoe asks. "I mean, my parents say it's a bunch of awful coincidences, or maybe poor old Clooney is losing it."

"I don't think so," I say. "She's barely taller than me, and I couldn't bump into the temperature dial in that cooler. And besides, she's loaded that dishwasher a gazillion times. No. It's not her."

"I agree with Quinnie," Ella says. "I'm up for checking out Baldy's place."

"So here's the plan," says Dominic. "Three of us go in, two of us stand guard. Quinnie, Zoe, and I will be on the inside, and Ben and Ella will hang outside. Sound good?"

"Me? Break into Hubert's?" Zoe's getting flustered. "What if we get caught?"

"We won't get caught," I say.

"But what if we do?" Zoe says. "And break in? Like break a window!?"

"Bad choice of words," I say. "No one is breaking any of those shiny new windows. But even though the front of the building has all new windows, the back has the old Loney Lobster Pound ones. I'm betting those don't even have locks, or if they do, they're old and rusted." I'm getting a little frustrated.

"The locks could be rusted shut," says Zoe.

"Or they could be rusted open," says Dominic. "It's the channel side of the building. It takes a beating from the salt air."

"Hey, if Rubylocks doesn't want to do it, I will," Ella says.

Ben and Dominic laugh. Zoe's cheeks flush almost to the color of her hair, and it looks like she's going to blow.

"Okay, okay," I jump in to calm her down. "First of all, Zoe, we love your hair. And Ella, that's great. If you want to go in, and Zoe, you want to stay outside with Ben, that's great. It's all good."

Zoe's eyebrows knit together. I know that look. She's struggling. She doesn't want to go inside, but also doesn't want to give it over to Ella. "Whatever. I'll go in. Somebody just tell me what to do, okay? But I'm not breaking anything."

I breathe a sigh of relief. "Good."

Dominic wipes his forehead and adjusts his cap. "Good. So we're set for tonight."

* * *

We gather on the beach behind Zoe's temporary house at two a.m. The moon's almost full, so it feels like there's a spotlight on us. We duck as we walk along the rocks, even though you can't dodge moonlight. Everyone is dressed in black, except Zoe, who's wearing a bright yellow hoodie and letting her hair fly like a freak flag. Wild red locks, yellow shirt? Not exactly stealth colors. I pull the scrunchie out of my hair and thrust it at her. I'm a little more nervous than I thought I'd be.

"What?" Zoe says.

"We're going stealth-style."

"Oh, sure. Right." She pauses and scoops the copper colored mass into a low ponytail.

Ella opens a small plastic pot of gray eyeshadow and smudges each of us under the eyes to promote invisibility.

We sneak beside the Maiden Rock Spiritual Center and up the center's drive. Our plan is to reach Restaurant Hubert from the long way around, past the Maiden Rock historical marker, Ms. Stillford's, and the bed-and-breakfast.

"Did you bring the flashlight?" I ask Dominic. My gut is knotting up.

"Check," he says.

"Camera?"

"Check."

As we're approach the B&B, which is the building nearest Restaurant Hubert, we hear voices and stop dead in our tracks. The knot tightens. We listen intently and realize it's summer people, sitting on the porch, chatting into the night. This presents a problem, since we can't walk past them. We're forced to plunge into the forested island in the center of Circle Lane, across from the B&B.

We try not to make too much noise as we thrash through the bushes toward Hubert's. Fortunately, the trees are dense, and the porch people are cheery enough that they don't notice us. If they had looked across the street, they would have seen a few wiggling balsam firs.

Soon we're crouched down in the thicket across from Hubert's. "Ready?" I whisper to Dominic and Zoe.

Zoe says, "This is a bad idea." She pauses, looks at Ella, and adds, "But I'm in."

"We'll watch the apartment above the restaurant," Ella says, "and text you if a light comes on."

"You mean Hubert *lives there*?" Zoe asks. "Great."

"Where else would he be?" Ben says. "Look, the lights are out. He's got to be snoring away."

We hunch over and scurry across the road and

along the side of the building. The scraping of our shoes against the grit and sand seems like it's echoing all over town. I try to put less weight on each step.

Our backs are against the building as we scoot toward the kitchen door. Dominic reaches up and tries the knob. He shakes his head. No surprise there.

Zoe whimpers.

My gut knot squeezes in on itself. We'll have to try a window. We move around the back, the side that hasn't been remodeled. Another deep breath. I remind myself that I expected it would be a window. I look to the windows on the second floor. Still dark.

Here at the back of the restaurant, they have left the old windows—the crank-out type. We start checking them.

Dominic's hunch has been proven correct. The back windows technically have locks, but they look like they rusted over in the open position a long time ago. I guess Owen Loney never had to worry much about lobster thieves.

The first window is cranked shut—and tight. The second one is not as tight, but we can't quite get our fingers in it. Dominic takes a screwdriver out of his pocket—he really thought of everything—and tries to wiggle it under the windowsill. Zoe looks like she's preparing to throw a hissy fit, so I press her arm and whisper, "Give him a chance."

There's a creaky sound, then a slight cracking noise around the edges as the window opens. We have access.

I boost a grumbling Zoe onto the nearest trash bin, and hoist myself up. The bin stinks like dead fish. On the other side of our lucky window, we find a mudroom and broom closet area.

I whisper to Zoe, "Move quickly and carefully. Look for anything that might be incriminating."

"Like what?" she whispers back.

"I don't know!" I say. She has no instincts for this stuff. "You just have to look at everything with an eye for a connection to Gusty's. And if you find anything unusual, call me. Don't touch it. It could be evidence. Got it?"

She squints. "Not really."

Dominic is already picking through a broom closet cabinet filled with soaps, detergents, and mops. I tiptoe through the mudroom in search of the pantry or the desk where they pay the bills. Zoe sticks her head into the kitchen.

My breath catches when I find a small office. I carefully move papers around a messy desk, my hands shaking, as I search for anything suspicious. I jump when my pocket vibrates with a text.

Ella: *Light on upstairs!*

Oh, no. I rush to find Dominic and tell him to hide, then speed to the kitchen to grab Zoe, who is . . . looking at spice bottles in an upper cabinet. And smelling one of them! *What the heck is she doing?* I *pssst* to her, and she puts it away and walks over. I pull her down behind the end of a row of cabinets.

A second later, feet thump on the stairs, and a figure saunters into the kitchen. It's dark but not so dark you can't make out Hubert. With the moonlight shining through the windows, those ears are a dead giveaway. He makes his way to the refrigerator and yanks open the big door, breaking the suction with a *pffft*. The fridge's interior light floods over him, casting a wide beam across his bald head and the prep island behind him. He's wearing boxer shorts and a stretched out T-shirt. He stares, yawns, and scratches his chest.

Zoe and I squeeze farther back into the shadows. He shouldn't be able to spot us now—but if the overhead light goes on, we're busted. I'm worried he can hear my low, slow panting. Zoe is digging her fingertips into my arm.

Hubert reaches into the refrigerator, takes out a large plastic bag filled with crabs, and sets it on the island. Then he reaches for the half gallon of milk behind it. With one hand, he takes off the cap, and with the other he glug-glug-glugs at least a quart of it. There's milk on his shirt, his face, and the back of his hand when he's done. The refrigerator's compressor kicks on, telling Hubert he should shut the door. He does, putting the carton back into the fridge but leaving the crabs on the counter.

Going by moonlight once again, he starts making his way around the kitchen, but this time, he's heading in an opposite direction—our direction. I don't know if I'm actually going to spontaneously combust, but it feels like I might. I clamp my hand over Zoe's mouth and feel her hot breath. We can't make ourselves any smaller.

Hubert's halfway around the kitchen island when he stops, grabs a spray bottle, and turns back in the other direction, toward the stairway. Just before he goes upstairs, he pauses in front of a potted herb plant and spritzes it with water.

When the apartment upstairs goes quiet, we beat it out of there.

As we pound down the beach on the way home, I assess what we found out—nothing.

But at least I can call this a clean getaway.

15

By the next afternoon, Ella, Dominic, Ben, Zoe, and I have worn ourselves out talking about the lack of evidence against Hubert, so the five of us decide to go sailing. We have Ben's uncle's boat and Zoe's parents' boat, everything we need for a race around the Maiden Rock Tidal Pool.

We're piling things into the boats before the race begins, and Zoe and I are laughing about Hubert's milk mustache, when we hear a sound you rarely hear in Maiden Rock—a siren.

We all turn to see an ambulance in full emergency mode fly down Mile Stretch Road, followed by Mom's squad car, its lights flashing too. We run to the other end of the dock and watch as the vehicles screech to a halt in front of Restaurant Hubert. We abandon the sailboats and sprint to the scene of the action. Mom's getting out of her cruiser as we arrive.

"Stay back, kids," she orders. People are jostling each other to get out of the restaurant. A paramedic team rushes in with a stretcher and comes out a minute later carrying a man who won't lie still. He's holding a plastic bag and heaving. A minute after that, the wild parade disperses and cars pull away, leaving the restaurant empty of patrons. We peek through the open front door and see Hubert slapping his head and yelling at Slick, who is screaming back at him. Chairs are turned over. Servers dressed in black pants, gray shirts, and dark red ties stand idle.

We head to Gusty's, where customers have wandered into the parking lot, standing around speculating about what just happened up the road. Dad's among the crowd, on his phone, no doubt talking to Mom.

"We saw it, Dad," I tell him.

"I guess someone got sick, huh?"

"Oh yeah, and an ambulance came, and people were running out of the restaurant."

"It was crazy," Ben says.

"Awful," says Zoe.

"Kind of cool," says Dominic.

Dad walks back into the café. "That's too bad."

I'm on his heels. "Well, it sure cleared out Hubert's."

"Heck of a way to do it." Dad shakes his head. "Come on, you guys must be hungry."

I groan. "You didn't see what we saw."

* * *

Ben reminds us the boats are waiting, so we head back to the yacht club. The planks on the pier are warm under my feet, and flies are buzzing around a dead fish that's smacking against the dock, reminding us that we'd better get going or the tide will go out and ruin our adventure. Zoe's parents' boat rocks as I step into it, and the sight of the poor heaving man flashes through my mind. "I wonder what made him sick?" I say.

"The raw beets?" says Zoe.

"The poaching liquid?" says Ella.

"The beam of light?" says Dominic.

It's a lazy, hull-bumping, name-calling couple of hours. I lie back and look at the sky and feel the cool sunny air blowing across my skin. Dominic and I are in a boat with Zoe, and Ella's in the other boat with Ben, and all is calm for this suspended moment. As I close my eyes and float along, I feel a tickle on my wrist. I don't have to open my eyes to know that Dominic is running his finger along the top of my hand the way he always does.

A text interrupts the joy of the moment.

Mom: *Home now. ASAP.*

My heart does a double beat. OMG—what's happened?

Zoe gets a similar text from her mom, telling her to report to my house—to my mom—and then immediately home.

She freaks. She can't get the boat back to the dock fast enough. Once we're there, we half walk, half run.

"This has to be about last night," Zoe says. "It has to be."

"No, it doesn't. Stop. You're getting me freaked out."

We're two doors away from my house when Hubert bursts out of our front door and lets it slam shut behind him.

We shriek simultaneously and stop in our tracks.

He jumps in his car and speeds away, his rear tires spitting up gravel and sand all over us.

Okay. Maybe Zoe's right. It's possible that, just maybe, this could be about last night. My mind traces our steps from the time we eased open the window until the time we pushed it shut. I can't think of anything we did that could have exposed us.

I feel Mom before I see her. She's radiating anger from her office all the way to our front steps. We find her in her sheriff's chair, her back to us, looking at her computer. I don't really want to announce that we're here, but I have to. "Mom?"

She doesn't turn around. "Is Zoe with you?"

"Yes."

"Come here."

"There?"

"Yes. Come look at my monitor, right now." Her voice is steely.

Zoe and I hold hands as we walk toward her. I haven't reported to a parent in this posture in a very long time.

Mom motions us into the office's two guest chairs, then starts a video.

It's dark. I can't make out anything for a second. Then my eyes adjust, and I swallow hard. There's moonlight. There's Hubert's kitchen. There's the top of my head as I sneak into the office. There's Zoe. At first, she's skulking around with her head at counter-top level as she looks in the lower cabinets. Then, as she moves through the room, she stands up taller and taller until she's just casually walking around, opening cupboard doors and looking at things. There's an especially good angle on her sticking her nose into a bottle of some spice. If there was any doubt that the footage caught me sneaking into the Restaurant

Hubert office, it definitely captures Zoe's massive, unmistakable ponytail in the kitchen.

I'm starting to feel the way that sick man at Hubert's looked.

Zoe's breathing hard, like she's wearing scuba gear.

Mom shuts off the footage and sits quietly. This must be some kind of interrogation technique—wait for the suspects to crack. It works.

Zoe starts blubbering.

I decide to be patient, just like Mom, and see what happens. Technically, I haven't done the thing she expressly prohibited me from doing—going around accusing Hubert of sabotaging Gusty's.

Finally she says, "I laughed." I relax a little. She continues, "I laughed at Hubert Pivot when he told me that you kids had broken into his kitchen and sabotaged the food and that's how the man got so sick today—"

I try to interrupt, "We didn't—"

"Be quiet, Quinnie. I laughed when he said this because I knew that was ridiculous. Impossible. Inconceivable. I laughed until he handed me this footage from his surveillance camera and told me to play it." She's speaking precisely in that way that leads to one of her rare flip-outs.

"But, Mom—"

"Then I *did* play it." She isn't even trying to control her anger.

Zoe's hanging her head, dripping tears on her shirt. "I just smelled some stinky spice!" she cries.

"Hubert's saying that whoever we see in this footage, messing around in the kitchen, has made his patron ill and damaged his reputation," Mom says. She digs a pad out from the pile of papers on her desk and picks up a pen. "Let's talk about how this happened."

She's serious. Mom's not just peeved at a couple of dumb-acting kids. She's a sheriff, about to take a statement from her suspects. My belly has never sunk so low.

"Zoe, you start," Mom says. She's going for the weaker of us first. The one most likely to spill her guts. I'm helpless until it's my turn. "Who all is involved? Tell me blow by blow: who, what, when, and where."

Zoe starts to fidget, looking at me like she thinks she might have said something wrong—and she hasn't even started. Of course, she can't help herself. "We pushed open an unlocked window and crawled in," she says. "It was the broom room. Dominic stayed there."

"Hold it. Dominic was there with you two?"

"Uh-huh."

"What about Ella and Ben?"

Zoe hesitates a second and then says, "They weren't there."

Mom tilts her head like she's trying to decide if she believes this, then picks up her phone and calls Dad. "Is Dominic at the café? Good. Send him to my office. I'll text his parents in a minute. Thanks." She turns back to Zoe. "Okay, keep going."

Zoe takes a deep breath and continues. "Quinnie went to the office, and I went into the kitchen. I walked around and looked at things. The only things I touched were the spice bottles and the handles on the cabinets. Then we heard footsteps, and Quinnie and I hid down by the end of the cabinets."

I am itching to jump into this, but I don't dare.

Zoe speeds up. "Hubert walked down in his underwear and went to the refrigerator and—"

Mom's jaw is dropping.

"—and he opened the refrigerator and drank from the milk carton and wiped the milk off his mouth and slapped his stomach and squirted a plant with water and went back upstairs."

Mom swallows. "Did you touch any food?"

We both say, "No!"

"You two better hope he doesn't want to press charges," Mom says, "because what you did was trespass, even if you didn't touch any food. And you better hope the man who got sick gets better. A sick customer could drive a restaurant out of business. And Hubert could say that the Buttermans are responsible for monetary damages."

Zoe crumples with her head in her hands.

My mind is going over the scene again and again, frame by frame, trying to think of what we might have touched. The refrigerator door? No. The bag of crabs? No. The carton of milk? *Wait.* The bag of crabs! He didn't put it back in the fridge.

"Mom, Mom—"

"Hold on, Quinnette." She puts her hand out to quiet me. "Zoe, did Hubert come down to the kitchen before or after the video I just showed you on the screen?"

"After. It happened after, and then we left."

"Mom. Mom. Mom—"

She turns to me. "Okay, your turn."

"He took something out of the refrigerator and didn't put it back."

"What?" Mom asks.

"A big plastic bag of crabs. And he didn't put it back."

"What time was this?" She's interested in this.

"It had to be about two a.m."

She makes a note. "Was the air on in the kitchen?"

Good. Now I know she gets it.

"No, Mom, it was warmer inside than outside. It was cold last night." This is the truth about summer in Maine. It still gets chilly at night, even after the sunny warmth in the daytime. "So those crabs sat out in the kitchen all night, and he cooked them and served them to that man. That's what made the guy sick."

She's mulling this over when I go for it. "Mom, we were only looking for evidence. Hubert's behind the bad stuff happening at Gusty's, believe me."

"Quinnie, stop it. You've got all the trouble you need right now. Go up to your room. Zoe, go home."

As Zoe and I leave the room, Mom picks up her phone, dials, and waits for an answer. "Hubert, this is Margaret Boyd. I want the last twenty-four hours of footage. Unedited."

16

I'm not saying Zoe and I are totally let off the hook, because we did sort of, kind of, actually, technically *trespass*, but Mom does talk to Hubert again after she's interviewed Dominic. I listen at her office door to her side of that call.

"Have you looked at the footage?" Mom asks in her sheriff's voice. "Well. I'm going to strongly suggest that you do that and then give me a call back."

After that comes the sound of Mom rocking in her chair. She must have ended the call. I guess she's giving Hubert a chance to put two and two together and realize he may have cooked bad crabs.

I go upstairs and text Dominic.

Me: *Where are you now?*

Dominic: *At home, waiting to be sentenced. Want to sit on the steps?*

Me: *Bad idea right now.*

Dominic: *Come on, you have never not wanted to sit on the steps. There's only so much step time left.*

This is killing me, and I'm not sure why I'm even saying no. I want to sit on those steps and touch shoulders and be less freaked out and have the last handholds of warmth, but that's all just going to make me cry and look dumb. I don't want to cry again. I need to stay focused. I've got to protect Gusty's, and I've got to toughen up and get ready for lonely hands.

Me: *She told me to stay in my room.*

Dominic: *Okay. Keep me posted.*

Ugh. I feel a little hurt from Dominic in that text.

* * *

At bedtime, I hear Mom and Dad talking in their room. The door is closed, so I creep up and, with my ear to the crack, listen to their worried conversation. Their voices are hushed and serious.

"I'll tell you what, Margaret, when I close the books for June, it's going to be brutal. The inspection, the dishwasher, the cooler, the power, people eating at Hubert's . . ."

"There's more traffic, right?" Mom asks. "I mean, the contest is bringing in more people. Isn't it?"

"Sure. But even with that, it's a net loss this month."

"At least you're not poisoning people," Mom says. The bed springs squeak like she's getting under the covers.

"What the heck happened with that?" Dad asks. "What did Quinnie have to say for herself?"

"After I told Hubert to look at the footage, he called me back. He's backing off pressing any charges against the kids. I think he realized what happened with the crabs and that the girls saw it. Suddenly he wants the issue all over with, short and sweet. All I can say is, if the girls hadn't seen him leave those crabs out, they would be in a world of trouble."

"I wonder how much this is going to cost Hubert," Dad says. "I'm sure that will turn out to be an expensive dish of crabs."

"Never mind that—what are we going to do to Quinnie?" I can imagine Mom shaking her head as she says this. "I mean, I told her she couldn't go out, but long term—what do we do?"

"She's got instincts for trouble, like her mother. Maybe she'll go to college for law enforcement."

"Oh my gosh, Gus. She's fourteen. First she needs to survive high school without getting thrown into a juvenile center or worse."

"Relax," Dad says. "Sometimes kids just get into stuff, play pranks, you know."

"This wasn't a prank. She's worried about Gusty's. And I'm worried about what she does when she gets worried."

The light goes off under their door, and I pad back to my room. Once I'm there, I open the window a crack and let the Atlantic air in. There's something about the waves hitting the rocky beach at night. Even when clouds don't let the moonlight through, the surf is still frothy white. It's familiar. It's normal. Unlike my life right now.

Thankfully, I'm not getting charged for breaking and entering, but I still feel in my bones that someone's up to no good in this town. Until this moment, I was convinced it was Hubert, that he was trying to make life miserable for Dad, but now I'm not sure. He can't seem to keep his own restaurant under control. My fingers are itchy. I have to blast out a group text.

Me: *So maybe it's not Hubert.*

Zoe: *I refuse to talk about this.*

Ella: *We can't just stand by and watch Gusty's get run out of business.*

Ben: *What would happen if Gusty's shut down? Would you still live here?*

This socks me in the gut.

Me: *Of course we would! My mom's the sheriff, the mayor, the real estate lady and the postmaster. We ARE Maiden Rock.*

Zoe: *What would your dad do?*

Ben: *He could hang around and drink coffee with Owen Loney.*

I don't think Ben was intending to knock the wind out of me again, but he did.

Dominic: *They could come to New Jersey and live with us.*

My eyes water at that.

Ella: *They can't leave Maiden Rock. They can live with us.*

Zoe: *They would live with us, first. I think. We've known them our whole lives.*

Me: *We're not going anywhere! Gusty's is not getting run out of business. We are going to save it.*

Zoe: *I'm not doing any more break-ins. I am not going to jail.*

Dominic: *I'll go to jail with you Q.*

Ella: *Me too.*

Ben: *I guess I will too.*

Zoe: *I'll write you guys.*

17

The next morning, Mom slaps an unofficial restraining order on me, Zoe, and Dominic.

"I'm almost running out of ideas as to how to get through to you about your"—she draws her lips tight and pauses before she says—"investigative nature. It seems like I tell you and you agree, and then a split second later, you're doing the very thing I thought we agreed you wouldn't do."

"Could I—"

"Wait."

"But—"

"You are not to go within fifty feet of Restaurant Hubert. This will apply to you, Zoe, and Dominic. Do you understand?"

"Yes."

"And let me add that the places you *can* go are each other's houses, the beach, Ms. Stillford's, Gusty's, and the yacht club. Anyplace else—if there's any doubt—you *ask* first. Got it?"

"Got it," I mumble.

I get the point. I could have been in really big trouble after crawling into Hubert's like that. But it's really going to handicap my investigation.

So we lay low for the day. We hang out at Gusty's, eat chowder and CBTs, and keep our eyes open.

"Okay, so maybe we're wrong," says Dominic. A strand of cheese from his Gusty's grilled cheddar-bacon-tomato sandwich stretches out over his chin.

The first six days of competition are over, and despite the problems, things actually look pretty good for Dad. At dinnertime, he's bopping around the café, smiling at everyone and being Gusty. Still, from my spot at my usual table, I'm watching everything with an eagle eye. I keep my back to the wall so I can see the parking lot, the whole dining room, the counter area, and a little of the kitchen.

Mr. and Mrs. Morgan, longtime summer people, have come in with their grandchildren, who have grown a year bigger but stayed noisy and loud. "I want a whoopie pie, Grandpa!" "No. Eat your blueberry pie." "Noooooo!" "Yes." "No." "Why not?" "Because it's not really blue." "Oh, for heaven's sake."

One table over, there's a young family with a toddler who's making a mess on the table that's spilling to the floor.

Mrs. Billingsley and Groucho are at the table next to them. She's giving the Morgan grandchildren and the toddler dirty looks and feeding lobster fries to the dog. When Dad stops by her table, she tips the butter cup and says, "This really needs to be heated to stay warm throughout the meal." Dad says, "It's a paper cup." She replies, "You could get those little contraptions that put a small candle under it." Dad repeats, "It's a paper cup."

The Lewises are here too. She's eating fish head soup and doesn't seem to be bothered by the fish head staring at her from the center of the bowl. He's eating a Gusty burger but asks to taste the soup. She wants a bite of the burger. They're kind of cute, the way they eat off each other's plates. I look at Dominic and wonder if we could do that. He's stuffing the last bite of his CBT into his mouth. I think that's a new record, five minutes for a giant sandwich. No, I don't see us picking off each other's plates. I'd starve.

Lone Man shows up again. He's dressed the same way as always—the fancy side of office casual. Light-colored striped shirt, khaki pants, loafers. I know he doesn't live in Maiden Rock, but he's been coming here a lot lately, although he's stopped with the picture-taking. This could make him the Secret Diner, or . . . it could make him a suspect in the assault on Gusty's. Hmm.

Clooney is knocking herself out to please him, which is so unlike Clooney. Maybe *she* still believes he's the Secret Diner too.

"More coffee?" Clooney asks Lone Man.

"Sure, I'll take a warm-up."

"How'd ya like that fish head soup? Pretty special, right?" she says as she picks up the empty bowl.

"Just superb," Lone Man says and wipes his mouth with his napkin.

Clooney beams with pride.

Lone Man continues: "Is that contest with the place up the street still going on?"

Clooney leans back and looks at him with a combination of confusion and suspicion. I can guess exactly what she's thinking: *Is this a trick question?*

"Well"—she starts slow—"yes. It is. It's going on for another ten days or so." Clooney looks around for Dad, but his back is to her. "Say, where did you say you were from?"

"Me? Oh, I'm from the Portland area."

"What you doing around here?"

"I'm an architect. I'm working on a project in Rook River for a couple months, and I just went exploring toward the shore and stumbled on Maiden Rock. What a quaint town. A real classic."

"That it is," says Clooney. She doesn't look convinced one way or the other about the origins of Lone Man now, but I see her attentiveness fade just a little bit.

Still, Dad takes his turn to schmooze. He swings by with a tray that has several plates of blueberry pie on it. "Can I tempt you?" he asks Lone Man.

"Sure." Lone Man pats his side. "I can't say no to that."

Dad makes his way to our table and lowers the tray. "Anyone for blueberry pie?"

Dominic reaches for one. I'm waiting on a whoopie pie myself. But before I can place my dessert order, the door opens and Sisters Rosie and Ethel arrive. Dad looks at the two remaining pieces on his pie tray and says, "Ah, there are my takers."

Cherubic Sister Rosie swoops up on Dad. "Dibs on those two!"

"They're yours," Dad says.

I ask the sisters to have a seat with us.

As Sister Rosie situates herself, she digs into the pocket of her flowing black skirt and pulls out a piece of paper. "I've been meaning to give you this, Gus. It's a recipe for a vegetable dish." She unfolds it and reads, "Corn—fresh corn, right off the cob—with heavy cream, green chilies, and buttered crumbs."

Dad pats Sister Rosie's hand. "Thanks for the recipe, Sister."

I check out Lone Man, whose pie plate is clean. He's scanning the room with that *where's my server?* look. He tries to get Clooney's attention but fails.

Mrs. Billingsley grumbles that she can't get her bill. Groucho romps on the floor, pulling on his leash with his teeth and jumping around like a flea. Dang, I want to play with that little guy.

Clooney can see Lone Man perfectly well, but you'd never know it. She's perfected that gaze servers have—it goes right past him. She's whispering to Owen Loney, who's holding down his stool at the counter. He has his ear tuned to her, but at the same time, he's watching Lone Man. I look back at the guy. He puts his napkin on the table and checks his phone for the third time. Again with the phone. There's an unease about him. He straightens his collar like he feels he's being watched.

What was it Monroe Spalding said in that one book by Ella's dad? *When a person thinks he's being watched, he's probably worth watching.*

18

The rest of the evening is calm, except for a notion brewing in my head: that Lone Man is not the Secret Diner but instead something more sinister—a perpetrator on Hubert's payroll. I don't mention it yet to anyone, because I need to observe him more closely and gather a shred of evidence. I wonder what other pictures he might have on his phone.

I fall asleep with visions of Lone Man breaking into Gusty's with some kind of lock-picking device and switching dish soap for dishwasher soap, then coming back to raise the cooler temperature. I have to laugh, because in my scenario, he's dressed like in a movie, with a black stocking cap, gloves, and a flashlight, creeping around on his toes.

I wake to my door flying open.

"Get up, Quinnie. Hurry. We need help. Dad needs help."

"What?" I grab for the covers. My eyes search for something that will tell me the time. What's going on? How bad is this? The sky outside says it's barely dawn.

"Something's happened at the café," Mom says.

"What do you mean?"

"Come on. Your dad will be here any second."

I stumble out of bed.

"Get dressed, come downstairs. Dad will pick you up so you can help Clooney put things back together." Then she's out of the room, leaving the whiff of freshly laundered sheriff's uniform behind her.

This is not like Mom. She's not one for being cryptic. What do I have to help fix? I search all at once for my jeans, a T, and my shoes. I check the phone for emails and texts. Nothing.

Dad's coming through the front door. He stops and holds it open. His face is as red as cayenne pepper.

I look at Mom. She waves her phone. "Go! Go!"

Getting in the car with Dad, I can feel the heat he's generating over whatever has happened. He must have assumed Mom told me, and she must assume he's going to tell me, but he keeps pounding the steering wheel with the heel of his hand and shaking his head, so I don't say a thing. Not one word.

"I need this like I need a hole in my head," he says.

We're rocketing down Mile Stretch Road on a white-knuckle ride until Dad does a left turn on two wheels, a la Sister Rosie, into the Gusty's parking lot. "Let's go."

I follow him around the back of Gusty's and through the kitchen door. Clooney is aproned, flour-covered, and frazzled. Dad points to the cabinet with the café's spices. "Can you get this straightened out?"

I have no clue what he's talking about. Straighten out the spices? Okay. I shimmy behind Clooney to the spice cabinet next to the griddle. She growls at me—actually growls. These two are really maxed out on the stress-o-meter.

"And when you're done with that, put the flour back where it belongs," Dad grumbles over his shoulder as he rolls out cinnamon buns.

I start to see why Dad's upset. The spices are a mess. All the caps are scattered around the shelf like they've been thrown in rage. It looks like someone has stuck their nose in all of them. I start by putting the caps on. When that's done, it feels safe to ask, "Do you want them in alphabetical order?"

"No, Quinnette!" Clooney is up in my face. "We want the right labels on the right containers!"

The right labels? What the what? I pick up the cinnamon and smell it. *Pew.* That's not cinnamon. That's . . . I'm not sure what, but it smells more like chili than gooey sugary buns. I pick up another one. It says paprika. I stick my nose in it and immediately sneeze. Ouch. It's red pepper.

I turn to Clooney with the paprika jar in one hand and the cinnamon in the other. "These are all wrong!"

She snarls. "That's supposed to be news to me?"

"Well, it's news to me!" I tell her.

"Ya don't say." She turned and yells to Dad, who's gone into the pantry. "Gus, ya better come in here."

Dad comes out wiping his flour-covered hands on a towel. "What now?"

I'm still holding the not-paprika when I say, "Dad! Who did this?"

There is so much emotion behind his eyes, I immediately regret the question. This is no accident. It can't be passed off as forgetfulness or lack of maintenance. A person did this, and Dad has to face it and he doesn't want to. "I don't know, Quinnie." He uses the back of his hand to scratch his forehead, leaving a white streak. It mixes with the sweat on his skin and makes a white sheen. "And I don't have time to think about it now. Can you just help fix it?"

All of a sudden it hits me. *He thinks I did this! That's why he came and got me!*

"Of course I'll fix things, Dad. But I want you to know I didn't do it. You and Mom could've grounded me for the rest of my life because of Hubert's kitchen. I would still never have done something like this. I would never hurt Gusty's."

I probably should just correct the labels and wait until Dad's cooled down before stating my case, but the point really needs to be made. "Dad, this was done by the same person who mucked up the dishwasher and raised the temperature in the cooler. This was done by your competition."

"What are you saying?" Clooney asks.

"I'm saying, whoever did this wants Gusty's out of the way."

Dad raises his white hands. "The flour, too?"

I don't know what he's talking about. "What about the flour?"

"Whoever was screwing up the spices also mixed a bunch of cornstarch with the flour and got a lot of dirt in it in the process. We lost an entire batch of buns before we realized it."

"Oh, Dad. What can I do?"

He drops his arms and shakes his head slowly. "It would be a disaster if someone got sick on our food or if the inspector came and found all this."

His expression of defeat breaks my heart. I make a move toward him when Mom hustles through the kitchen door.

"Mom, listen. Please. Whatever has been going on is not accidental. This"—I point to the spices—"this was on purpose. And why spices? Because the wrong ones would make the food taste terrible. It had to be Hubert or his henchmen."

Mom's face cracks slightly. "Go on."

I take a deep breath and begin a calm and logical recitation of my concerns. "Look, up until now, you could say that everything that's happened was a coincidence—things breaking, pure accidents. But this? No way. Someone *did* this. And they did this to mess up Gusty's." I put down the red pepper jar with the paprika label that I've been clutching. "I know you don't want me to accuse Hubert or even Willy. Fine. But that doesn't mean someone else on the payroll isn't acting on their behalf."

Mom is about to interrupt me, so I hold up my hand and ask her to wait. "Who can deny that they have motive?" I continue. "It's possible, right?"

Mom settles down again.

I continue, cautiously. "So what if it's the man who's been in here the last few days? The one we've been thinking might be the Secret Diner? What if he's actually a spy for Restaurant Hubert?"

"Martin? Maybe he likes my food," Dad says and rolls his eyes.

"I don't know," Clooney says. "The kid may be onto something." She walks to the sink and washes her floury hands. "He asked me if the contest was still going on, and I asked just what was he doing in this town. And do you know what he said?" She dries her hands with determination. "That fella said he 'just stumbled on Maiden Rock.'" She points at Mom. "You know as well as I do, Margaret, nobody just stumbles on Maiden Rock. You gotta know it's here to find it."

"I can't disagree that this thing with the spices and the flour is no accident," Mom says. "Someone did this on purpose, with ill intent."

"And I don't know if this Martin is as nice as he first appeared," Clooney says. "He's gotten a little demanding."

"If Hubert's trying to send a message, he's gonna have a fight on his hands," Dad says. He puffs up. "I can be a Bangor bear when I have to be."

Mom's examining the back door now. "It's not damaged, but someone certainly got through it. Possible lock-pick situation. Don't touch it—may be too late, but I'll try to lift a print."

Before she leaves, she turns to Dad and says, "I'll call the locksmith and get him out here to put new keyed dead bolts on both doors as soon as he can." Then she beckons me over to her.

"I know it's useless to tell you not to poke your nose into this, but whatever you do, don't make me have to arrest you."

19

I knuckle down and start on the spice labels. Dad calls for a grocery delivery. Clooney opens the last thirty-pound bag of flour in the pantry and gets going with new dough. By the time Dad unlocks the front door, the traditional Gusty's smells are starting to waft out of the ovens. Late but not a complete miss.

Of course, the first person through the door is Owen Loney. He shuffles to his typical seat and drums his wrinkled lobsterman fingers on the counter. Dad sits down next to him with two cups of coffee.

"Mornin', Owen."

"Mornin', Gus."

"What can I get for you besides coffee?"

"Not a thing, Gus. Coffee'll do."

"You can't live on coffee, my friend. You're wasting away. You've got to eat something once in a while."

I'm listening to this conversation while I work on the spices, which requires interrupting Clooney constantly and asking her, "What's this one?"

"I'm not taking no for an answer," Dad says to Owen. "You order something or I'll bring you what I think you should eat. Come on. On the house."

Owen Loney grumbles then says, "Whatever. Fine, I'll take two eggs, side by each, and a pair of toast."

Dad pats him on the shoulder, and I feel a wave of goodness from both of them.

Once I'm done with the spice reset, I ask Dad and Clooney if there is anything else I can do for them. They say no and load me up with a bag of breakfast goodies: cinnamon bun, blueberry muffin, crab-cake-and-egg sandwich.

Before I leave, Dad pulls me aside. "I'm really sorry I was so harried this morning. This is all just so horrible."

"It's okay. Dad. I know. And I want to help catch whoever is doing this."

"I just wish—"

"I know. You just wish I wasn't so much like Mom."

He laughs. "Not at all. I love that you're like your mother. You two follow a mystery like a bloodhound after a rabbit." He gives me a big hug. "But leave this to her, will you? Today was very scary."

* * *

Six hours later, my friends and I are lolling on my back porch, watching the waves. We each have a leg over the arm of our chair. The scene would look casual from the outside, except everyone is quietly tense. The sun's beating on the beach rocks, but their hot, smooth surface will fake out anyone who thinks the water's going to be warm too. The Morgan grandchildren skip ahead of their grandparents, wearing swimming suits. Big mistake.

"I bet your mom traces this Martin guy's license plate number," says Ella.

"It could be a rental car," says Dominic.

Zoe says, "He doesn't look like a bad guy."

I sort of agree with her. "Maybe he's not," I say. I'm torn about this. "It could still be Slick or Hubert. Well, probably not Hubert himself. After watching his midnight milk-drinking mess, I don't think he can be stealthy. But it could still be Slick. Or anyone else. Anyone."

"The lock wasn't actually broken on the door, just released or tricked somehow," says Zoe. "That might mean a professional criminal." She tightens up and makes an *eek* sound.

"Or someone with a key," Dominic says. "Who has keys?"

"Dad and Mom and me and Clooney. That's all." I start to pace along the porch as I wonder who else could have gotten a copy of the key. "Anyway, we need to be more organized about our investigation."

Zoe groans. "No more playing detective, *please*."

I ignore her. "What if we stake out *both* restaurants and record who comes and goes? Then we compare findings, like who's been going to both of them?"

"We'd probably spot the Secret Diner too," Ella says.

"For sure," Ben says. "And when Gusty's is closed, let's have someone watching it. The front door and the back door, since I don't think crooks walk right in the front."

"Hang on." I pause to think this through a second. "My mom is ordering new super-locks for the café doors—"

"That doesn't mean he won't try—"

"I know, I agree. But I'm thinking *my mom* will have someone out there at night, like an unmarked squad car from Rook River. So let's stick to days as

153

long as she has that covered. Now, who's going to stand watch and fill in the report at each location?"

"I am not standing watch," Zoe says. "Nowhere, no how, no place."

"One minor consideration," Dominic adds. "The restraining order."

I wave off his concern. "No problem. Even if it were a hundred percent official, that only applies to three of us. Ben and Ella can go anywhere they want."

I run from the porch into the kitchen and return with a pen and paper. "Okay, so we need shifts at both places. And we don't have a lot of time. Tomorrow's day nine of the competition."

Ben and Ella take the Hubert's shifts. That's a given. Ella takes a.m., Ben p.m. I take mornings at Gusty's. Dominic takes through closing.

"I'll be your Gusty's backup," Zoe says. "From my window."

20

By the close of business, and after two and a half days of surveillance, my friends and I have a list of people going in and out of Restaurant Hubert, complete with dates and times, and we've cross-referenced it with people coming and going from Gusty's. We've also determined that Mom had a car at that location, confirming my hunch about a man in the field.

This hasn't been easy. It's the Fourth of July holiday, and the town's having its typical influx of strangers. That means extra license plates, along with changes to note in family composition, attire, and general behavior. Plus, we've been a little distracted by Dad's picnic menu, along with the clowns on the fire truck during Sunday's noon lunch hour (we went out to hoot).

By the close of the weekend, our list has about twelve persons of interest who've gone to both restaurants. Some we know by name. Some we can only describe. We get together on my porch to discuss the matches.

I chew on the end of a pen as I read our results from a spreadsheet that Dominic put together. "So, it's the young couple with the toddler with the messy face and hands; an old man with a walker who doesn't look like he'll make it through the week; Mr. and Mrs. Boardman, who are regular Maiden Rock summer people; Martin the Lone Man; the Lewises; Slick; Mrs. Billingsley; and—what—the sisters!?"

"Oh, your dad's not going to like Sister Rosie and Sister Ethel eating at Restaurant Hubert," Ella says.

"I think they're just curious." I tap my pen on their names.

"I don't know," Ben says and raises his eyebrows. "Maybe we should keep them on the list."

Ella and I look at each other for a long moment. "It's not like they're angels," she says. "But they do come into Gusty's every day. And they clearly love the place. And they've tried to help with these goofy recipes. What's their motive for being in cahoots with Hubert?"

"Maybe he's making a big donation to their cat-rescue fund?" says Ben.

Dominic laughs. "From what I hear, they have learned their lesson about fundraising."

"Really," Zoe says, "I can't see Sister Rosie as a cat burglar."

"Oh, yeah?" says Ben. "Sister Ethel's got some moves. I mean, she can handle a boat like a demon."

I decide to leave them on the list but put them at the bottom.

"What do we really think about these names? Do we need to watch them all?" Ella asks.

"We know Martin is a suspect," I say. "And Slick, for sure. And Mrs. Billingsley? If anything, she's punishing Hubert by also eating at his restaurant. Especially if she's telling him to warm the bowls or whatever too. Mr. and Mrs. Boardman are a 'no way.' They've been coming to Gusty's forever. The hundred-year-old man? He moves at the speed of a turtle. But the Lewises? I wouldn't have guessed the Lewises might make the suspect list. Still, we need to put eyes on them. Them and the messy toddler family."

"When you think about it," Ella says, "either of the messy toddler's parents are fit enough to manage a break-in. The toddler could be a decoy."

"Where do the Lewises live, anyway?" Zoe asks. "I don't think they're Maiden Rockers."

"I don't know," I say. "You know, they don't eat like normal people. They're always picking off each other's plates."

"People do that all the time," Ella says and gives Ben's leg a bump. "Ben eats most of my food."

Ben smiles. "Sure, but not till you're done with it."

Dominic says, "Between the Lewises and the toddler parents, I'm going with the toddler parents. They're more likely to be friends with Hubert, fit enough to sneak into the café and do the deeds, and smart enough to have jammy-kid cover."

I laugh at that last part, but Dominic is serious. "The kid is an authentic touch."

2I

I'm trying to be a professional about this. When the spreadsheet is cleaned up and I think it contains the most reasonable possible list of suspects—and the rest of my crew has headed back to their own homes—I go looking for Mom.

She's in her office, near the end of signing a lease. I wait quietly.

When she's done, she swivels her chair around and smiles. "What's up, kiddo?" I've been holding the investigative report behind my back, but she sees it. "What's that?"

I know better than to just hand it over. Instead, I give it a concise introduction. "Mom, I wanted you to know, because you always want me to tell you things, that my friends and I have not broken into any more places or violated our restraining orders. But we *have* made some observations that we think are useful in this investigation. I put them in this report."

She leans back in her chair. Her shoulders sag a little, although not as much as they might have. Which is a good sign. "Okay." She reaches for the report, and now I do hand it over. She studies the page as I start to explain.

"We made lists of everyone who went in and out of Gusty's and Hubert's and cross-referenced them. Then we narrowed them down to one list of people who have some connection to both places and might be the ones who are sabotaging Gusty's."

"Or who might be the Secret Diner?" Mom asks. "Right? Going to both places isn't necessarily incriminating. It could be the sign of a person trying both menus. Like the Secret Diner's supposed to." She looks at me for confirmation.

"True. But the person who's in on it with Hubert might have the same routine."

"I guess that's possible. But these people are only people who ate at both places, right? During business hours, during the time you surveyed?"

"Right. Business hours. We just looked for connections among people who came and went. Whether they ate or not once they went in, I don't know."

Mom looks at the list again. "You know, Quinn, I'm not dismissing the idea that there is a connection between Hubert and what's happened at Gusty's." She gazes out the window as she continues. "And tracking people eating at both places is one way to look for a connection. Still, I'm not persuaded that the person who broke in and tampered with things would have to be any of these people. But I have to admit . . ." She pauses and rocks in her desk chair. "None of this started until Hubert arrived."

"Okay, Mom, but my report—at least it identifies some possibilities, right? Or eliminates some people, right?"

"Sure. Is this list comprehensive?" she asks.

"Well, I eliminated some obvious people and . . ." I watch her read to the bottom.

Mom throws back her head and laughs. "Oh my gosh. Dad will be surprised to see the sisters on here."

"I know they've had their problems." I'm having second thoughts about leaving them on.

"You're right. But if there is one truth in this town, it's that those ladies love Gusty's and they would never do anything to hurt it. It would kill them to think your father knew they'd tried Hubert's food. How many times were they there?"

I consult my chart. "Just once."

"I think you can take them off before we show this to Dad." It gets another laugh out of us. "You know, Quinnie, the person doing this is probably not walking boldly into either restaurant—"

"But that could be the perfect cover!" I argue. "Hiding in plain sight."

"Yes. Yes. I agree. But remember, whoever messed with the spices, they did it at night. Not while Gusty's was serving lunch."

Maybe I'm about to raise Mom's temper, but I keep pushing. "If you had to pick a suspect from the list, though . . ."

She looks back down at the paper. "I can't say about the Lewises. I suppose it's possible. They look affluent. They don't live in town. They come frequently. They aren't very friendly. They could have some interest in Hubert's succeeding. But they don't exactly fit the profile for people who would do the dirty work."

"What about the people with the toddler? He could do it or she could do it."

"The Camps? I've seen them in Gusty's. They're both fit enough for a caper. And they look about Hubert's age. It's possible they have some connection. Maybe. Still, they don't fit the profile either."

"What about the rest?"

"'Martin' is Martin Candor of Fergusson Architectural Firm. I traced his license plate. It's a rental in the name of the firm. I think that eliminates him as a suspect. He could still be the Secret Diner, I suppose, but that would make him a very busy man. Willy Lovelace—I'm not calling him Slick—I shouldn't be telling you this, but he's got a short rap sheet. Bad checks, siphoning gas, driving while intoxicated. All when he was pretty young, though. Still, he could be doing this for money or out of misplaced loyalty. He's on my list."

I don't know why I'm always surprised by this, but Mom has been on the case all along. I want to snatch the investigation report back out of her hands and record this new info, but I remain calm and nod my head, trying not to show how overly interested I am.

"I don't think it's Hubert himself," Mom continues. "He'd have too much at risk just as a property owner here in Maiden Rock, and then there's his reputation. But I'm interested in the new inspector too. I'm checking him out."

Yes. Yes. Yes.

"At least the contest will end soon," she adds. "And who knows, maybe this will all be over after the winner is announced." She gets up and places the paper on her sheriff's desk. "Don't get any closer to this, okay? If you have an idea, come to me. This was good, what you did. But no closer. Messing with equipment, tainting the flour . . ." Her voice trails off. "This character could be dangerous."

* * *

I walk out of the room slowly, not wanting to rattle the whole house by pounding up the steps. Once I'm behind my door, I open up the spreadsheet that Dominic made and start arranging our suspects in order of most likely to sabotage Gusty's. The biggest revelation from Mom is that Slick has a record. This puts him back at the top of my list—after Hubert Pivot. I kind of see her point, that Hubert wouldn't do this himself, but still, he has the biggest motive. Motive, means, and opportunity. That's what a suspect needs.

In the number three spot, I take Mom's lead and put the new inspector. I debate whether Martin Candor or the Lewises should be in the fourth spot, then decide the toddler parents should go fourth. They're the most physically fit. Fifth place goes to the Lewises, because Martin seems to be a legit architect. But still, he's in sixth. I leave off the hundred-year-old man and Mrs. Billingsley. I just don't see either of them being involved.

With the names rearranged, I fall asleep feeling this case is well in hand.

* * *

The second I wake up, I text the group.

Me: *I gave my mom the list and she took it. She has her own suspects too.*

Ella: *?????? Tell.*

Dominic: *Lone Man Martin, right?*

Me: *Let's meet. My porch.*

Ella: *How about my porch? I don't have a sheriff in my house.*

Zoe: *How about my porch? It's never MY porch.*

Ben: *I'm in a bball camp in Rook River today.*

Dominic: *I have to help clean this rental house today—boo.*

Zoe: *Yeah. You better get all your germs out before I reclaim my room.*

Me: *Hello!*

This is getting ridiculous.

Zoe: *Actually I can't now. I have to go somewhere with my parents. I'll be gone all day. Tonight after dinner? Maybe we could do a sleepover on my porch. I'll make snacks. Totally cool Scottish snacks.*

Ben: *It won't be sheep intestines or bladders will it?*

Zoe: *Shut up. Of course not.*

Dominic: *Sounds good to me.*

Ella: *Fine. Whatever.*

All the patience is draining out of me. We're on the trail of something big here, and we're losing focus. On the other hand, a sleepover will give us the whole night to figure this out.

Me: *Okay. Done. Sleepover tonight at Zoe's.*

Zoe: *Uh, one more thing. I don't think my parents will allow Dominic and Ben to actually sleep over.*

Dominic: *Fine. We'll leave before midnight—before we turn into vampires.*

* * *

At eight p.m., Ella knocks on my door, and we knock on Dominic's door, and all of us head to Zoe's. Ben is already there, since he and his uncle were invited for dinner. Zoe's parents and Ben's uncle John have finished eating, and they're relaxing around the dining room table with their chairs pushed back. A few molasses cookies sit untouched on a flowered plate. Zoe's mom and Uncle John are talking about when they were kids and he made her a harness and wings out of a bedsheet and tied her to a tree limb. "Hey, she wanted to be Tinker Bell," he says. Zoe's mom nearly spits out her coffee.

The rest of us file through the kitchen and toward the porch, grabbing sodas while Zoe rounds up some bags of chips. Zoe's dad says loudly, "You kids keep it down out there!" This is followed by uproarious laughter from all three adults.

The Buttermans' current porch has delicate-looking furniture—no slamming into chairs or cramming pillows into balls under our heads for us. Zoe's parents have placed vases with flowers and citronella candles atop the small, round glass tables. We manage to get comfortable without full-on slouching.

"Can we light the candle?" Ella asks.

"I don't think so," Zoe answers.

I show everyone a printout of the revised suspect list.

"I agree Hubert-slash-Slick should be number one-slash-two," Ella says.

"Me too," says Ben.

"I don't think the people with the baby could be it," Zoe says as she breaks open three chip bags and pours them into a few bowls. "They seem nice and really have their hands full with the baby."

"Well, I for one still think that the messy toddler is a great cover," Dominic replies.

"I think the Lewises are suspicious," I say and reach for a chip and pop it in my mouth. It takes a couple seconds for the taste to register in my mouth. Then I spit the half-chewed pulp into my hand. "What is this?"

Ben and Dominic each reach for chips from the other bowls. Within a few chews, they are both moaning. Ella doesn't move to try the chips at all.

"You guys! These are great," Zoe says as she pops a few more into her mouth.

Dominic, who is the most adventurous eater among us, asks her, "What's on them?"

Zoe shows the fronts of the three bags: *Roddy's Haggis with Coarse Ground Pepper, Roddy's Highlands Ghost Pepper*, and *Roddy's Roasted Ox*.

The rest of us groan in unison.

Zoe's face is as red as her hair now. "You don't like them? Fine. I brought them all the way home from Scotland, where everyone loves them, and I opened these especially for you guys, and you . . ." Her voice trails off into what I know is going to be a tear fest.

"Wait, Zoe," I start. "Maybe we're just not used to them. You've had two years to get used to them. You must have thought they were weird the first time you tasted them . . . right?" I'm almost pleading with her not to become a huge overnight grump. I reach for an ox chip and nibble on the edge. I want to say, *That's not so bad*, but I can't.

Zoe looks at Ella. "Are you going to try them?"

"I don't even do Moxie much," Ella says apologetically.

"But you tried it," I say.

Ella gives me a green-lidded evil eye. "Only because it's the official drink of Maine. We're not in Scotland."

"Zoe, these chili pepper ones aren't bad," Ben says, "except they're destroying my taste buds for life and singeing the hair inside my nose. I can eat a few but I need like a gallon of milk."

I don't want to upset Zoe any more, but I really want to get back to talking about suspects.

Surprisingly, Ella come to the rescue. "If you have some Ziploc bags, I'll help you put them away, and they'll stay fresh like you never opened them."

The anger starts to fade from Zoe's face. She looks at Ella, then at the bowls, then at Ella. "Sure. Yeah. Thanks."

My blood pressure goes down too. When they get back from the kitchen, I'm forcing a discussion of what we should do next.

"Look, since Slick's first on the active suspect list,

I think he's the one to keep a close eye on. He's got all the signs of being our guy."

Ella offers, "Whenever Monroe Spalding's on a case, he says, 'It's the thing you don't think of that's most significant.'"

I ask, "You mean, if we're supposed to think they're nobody, then they're somebody, right?"

"Right."

"So the Lewises, the toddler family, that Martin guy, Mrs. Billingsley, and the hundred-year-old man are all real suspects . . . and Slick is not?"

"I don't know," Ella says. "Maybe. I'm just reporting what an experienced detective has to say on the matter."

"An experienced detective in a book," says Ben.

He may just be a detective in a book, I think. But he's been right before. I remind myself to keep my mind open.

22

The next day, we've switched our task from surveillance at outposts near restaurants to tailing specific suspects. Unfortunately, that still leaves Ella and Ben concealed in the bushes outside Restaurant Hubert. Because they're free from the informal restraining order, they've been assigned Hubert and Slick, and they keep texting us complaining about how detective work is a "whole lot of waiting around." I keep texting them back, "Suck it up." Zoe is watching Gusty's from her bedroom window, and Dominic and I are in my family's dining room, researching our new shorter list of suspects online.

"Look at this," he says and swivels his laptop in my direction. "Martin Candor really is an architect." There he is, on Dominic's screen, wearing his usual kind of plaid shirt and tan pants. He has a hardhat on his head and a rolled-up plan under his arm. Behind him is some renovated historic building in Augusta. "I can't see a reason for this guy to be involved with Hubert."

I stare at the picture for a few seconds. At first, I'm going to tell Dominic, *Let's not spend any more time on this guy*, but then it hits me. "See if he's the one who did the plans to turn Loney's Lobster Pound into Restaurant Hubert. Maybe they met that way."

"Good idea," Dominic says and digs in.

My thumbs are flying around on my tablet, inputting every phrase about cooking I can think of that would bring up info on Hubert Pivot.

"Oh my gosh, look at this! He had hair!" I show Dominic that patchwork of images that comes up on a Google search. In Hubert's case, there's chef's coats of varying colors, sparser and sparser hair, increased worry lines, looks of defiance, looks of exasperation, but never a real, full-on smile. I spot one photo with his characteristic smirk. But the more I study the gallery, the more I realize the smirk is not a smirk at all. He has a scar just above the left corner of his mouth, and it makes him look like he's curling his lip on his resting face. That's kind of a bummer for him.

Next, I try the links. Many of them lead to interviews. I click on one from last year.

At what looks like a fancy espresso shop, a reporter

with a big bulbous microphone says to the camera, "We are here at Café Encre Bleue with Hubert Pivot, the chef who has just dramatically walked away from a position at Shovela, a prestigious five-star restaurant, in order to preserve the integrity of his creative spirit." The camera pans to show the famous chef next to him. "Chef, what are your plans for the future?"

For someone who recently pitched a fit over the variety of kale in a salad, Hubert looks remarkably calm. He swallows, and his Adam's apple bobs up and down. "The natural variety of ingredients in the world is the essence of cooking. I cannot work where those distinctions are not appreciated."

The reporter with the big microphone looks surprised that Hubert's answer is so short. "Could you say more about what you'll do next?"

"Let me say one other thing first. I cannot abide the wasting of food. True chefs use all of the vegetable. They repurpose a misshaped and unloved tuber. At Shovela, they couldn't understand that."

"Are you contemplating a new signature dish?" The reporter thrusts the mic up a little higher, as if to urge Hubert to fill it up with enough words to cover the spot.

"I'm definitely exploring the spotted reef crab. It's a tiny, fingernail-sized crab that only grows on the west side of Oahu and must be harvested by divers who separate each one from the reef by hand."

The reporter presses him. "How will you prepare them?"

"You don't expect me to answer that, do you?" Hubert is dead serious.

"Ha, ha, no. I guess not. You guys have your secrets."

Hubert appears to lose interest, and I click on another link, this one leading to an episode of a public TV show that profiles young chefs. The episode's focused on Hubert Pivot. The studio kitchen is cramped but simple, with scaffolding behind and above the cooking area. The camera drifts around and sometimes catches audience members, light stands, and the backstage crew.

Hubert has half a head of hair and sports a classic white chef's coat. He speaks in low tones, and a crew member comes up and adjust the microphone and whispers to him.

"They're telling me to speak up," Hubert says, and a few titters arise from the audience. "So, let's see, today, I'm going to talk about myself, which I can't imagine many of you are interested in, and I'm going to do it while I make a tempeh dish. It's going to be like watching a trained bear spinning saucers on sticks while standing on one foot."

The audience laughs, which seems to perk Hubert up. He smiles a little. Finally.

He slices zucchini as he continues. "So I grew up reading cookbooks, and I enrolled in the Culinary Academy of North America as soon as I could, before I finished high school." He scrapes the chip-sized disks from the cutting board and drops them into sizzling hot skillet. "Of course, I didn't finish. Too many tests and things. I had to be in a restaurant kitchen." He lifts the pan from the flame and shakes it, flipping the slices into the air, then expertly catching them. He doesn't make eye contact with the camera. His eyes are on his knife as it turns basil leaves into frilly shreds. "I believe in fresh. I believe in organic. I believe in honest cuisine."

The camera pans the audience, and a few people in the front row are leaning forward to smell the food.

"Hey, Q, look at this!" Dominic grabs my sleeve and shoves his phone in my face. At the same time, my own phone starts going wild with texts.

Ben: *YOW the inspector is at Hubert's.*

Ella: *Yeah he's talking to Slick at the kitchen door.*

Ben: *We think Slick just gave the inspector something. Holy sheesh.*

Ella: *It looks like an envelope. Could be cash.*

Ben: *What should we do?*

I start typing like a fiend:

Me: *Are you getting this on your phones?!! Pics or movie whatever you can get.*

A few seconds later, I get a photo message from Ben. The picture shows Slick in the doorway with a white cloth tied around his waist. You can clearly see his face, and there's a burst of light shining off his left ear. The inspector's facing him, his back to us. Except for the fact that Slick's left shoulder is a little high and he's got a bent elbow, you can't see anything being passed between them. No envelope. No nothing. Another picture comes. There's a smile on Slick's face—he's slugging the inspector on the shoulder. These guys are getting along big time.

Me: *Don't go any closer.*

* * *

By lunchtime, Ella and Ben are done with their Restaurant Hubert surveillance shift, and we meet up at Gusty's. On the way in, we have to queue up behind the toddler family and Mrs. Billingsley. At least Billingsley's with Groucho. That little dog is so darn cute. Today, he's wearing little blue overalls. It's hilarious.

Mrs. Billingsley heads for the table she has made her own, all the while burrowing in her big hand-bag and grumbling that she can't find something. After some deep digging that attracts the attention of everyone in the café, she dumps the bag out on the table. A mountain of stuff appears: a wallet, a can of dog food, a ring of keys, wet wipes, the head of a flashlight. She brightens and picks up the head of the flashlight, which has a headband attached to it.

"Here we go, Groucho." She scoops up the little dog and puts the light on his head. Instantly, I realize he's a Minion. I can't help myself, I like Mrs. Billingsley a bit for dressing up her dog like a freakin' Minion.

That is, until she makes a great display of waving her arms in the air and telling Clooney that there's something sticky on her tabletop.

Without a word or a smile, Clooney walks over like a robot and wipes the tabletop with a wet cloth, using more circling motions than reason would call for. Then she wipes it dry. Before she turns away, she gives Groucho the Minion some good old down-east stink eye.

"What shall we have today, Grouchy?" Mrs. Billingsley asks the dog in a goo-goo baby voice.

At the next table, the toddler parents are way past baby talk. The dad is busy moving the salt, pepper, sugar, ketchup, and other tabletop condiments out of the toddler's reach. The mom pulls out a baggie with cheddar Goldfish and tries to keep the kiddo busy. He's crying and waggling his fingers toward the sugar packets. For a second, it looks like the dad is going to give in and let there be sugar and sweetener all over the table.

For once, Ben's more interested in talking about his observations than his stomach. Dominic and I listen intently.

"The inspector drove up kind of fast and jumped out of the car, still talking on his cell phone," Ben says. "As he was walking to the kitchen door, he ended the call and stuck the phone in his pocket."

"He was carrying a clipboard, like he was going to do official inspection business," says Ella. "But before he could go in, Slick came to the door and stepped out."

"Yeah, and Slick kept looking over his shoulder while they were talking, like he was watching to make sure no one inside saw him," Ben adds.

"He was looking around outside, too," Ella says. "Do you think you should show these pictures to your mom, Q?"

"The problem is," I say, looking at them again, "the really important parts aren't visible, like the inspector's expression and the transfer of the envelope."

"Hi, guys!"

I nearly jump out of my skin when Dad shows up at our table. We all ease back from our phone-watching positions. "Hi, Dad."

"What's it gonna be? Today's special is a Gusty burger, lobster fries, and a soda of your choice."

Ben stretches and rubs his stomach. "I'll have that, and some onion rings too, and a whoopie pie and milk."

Dominic says, "Clam chowder—a bowl, not a cup—and pie and Moxie."

"No fish head soup today?" Dad asks.

"It's really delicious. Really. But today I'm going with the *chowda*."

Dad scratches his head with the non-ink end of the pen. "Do you guys think I should serve it without the heads?"

"No, Dad!" I tell him. "It's perfect the way you have it on the menu. Just like it is now."

Dad nods noncommittally and wanders away, mumbling about how Hubert has him all bollixed up. I look at Ella, and we smile sadly. Poor Dad and his fish head dilemma.

23

For the rest of lunch, I wrestle with whether I should show the pictures to Mom. This could clinch our case that Hubert is bribing the inspector to harass Gusty's and that Slick is his go-between. Except, that's not exactly what they show. One captures Slick and the inspector friendly-like and goofing around. The other shows Slick talking to the inspector and smiling and moving his arm, plus a view of the inspector's back. You have to put the second image together with Ben and Ella's testimony to establish that an envelope passed between them. And the first thing Mom would say is, *But we don't know what's in the envelope.* And I'd want to whine a little bit and say, *What else could it be?* And she'd say, *That's circumstantial evidence and not very persuasive circumstantial evidence.* We need a real link.

I mull this over as I swallow my last bite of lobster

roll. Even if Willy is up to no good, the stuff in that envelope could have been money to bribe the inspector to give *Hubert's* a *good* health rating. I have no proof it relates to Gusty's. I'm pretty much concluding I should wait to show Mom the pics, when the café door opens and Martin Candor comes in. I almost forgot about him for a minute.

"Don't stare," Dominic whispers to me.

"Right," I say, but I keep checking him out. Same shirt, same pants. Same business casual clothes. He smiles. Not too small, not too large. Seems comfortable in his own skin. Waits casually for a seat.

Something comes over me, and I wave him to our table. "Over here, mister. You can sit here. We're leaving."

He raises his hand slightly as if to say hi and thanks at the same time.

We're filing past him when I get a burst of boldness. "Can I ask you a personal question?"

He reels back a bit but says, "Maybe. It depends on how personal it is."

"The first day you were here, I saw you take a picture of the café. Why'd you decide to do that?"

His brow wrinkles like he's trying to remember the first day he was here. Then he laughs. "Well, that's not so personal. I'm an architect. I like buildings—especially old café buildings like this one. You know, some people like barns. I like these."

"What do you mean?"

He takes out his phone and scrolls to the picture he took of Gusty's, then starts pointing to various spots on it. "The frame of the place is similar to many built during the postwar period . . ."

It starts to sound like blah blah blah blah de blah. I look to the door. Everyone's gone outside, except Dominic, who is giving me bug eyes. I wave at him to go ahead, then turn back to Martin Candor. "I'm Quinnie Boyd," I say and stick out my hand.

"Martin Candor." He shakes my hand. His hand feels like a normal hand. Not the hand of a saboteur. "Are you related to Gusty?"

"He's my dad."

"Well, Quinnie Boyd, you live in a very special town and you have a very special father. And this is a classic New England structure."

I leave the table pretty convinced he's not planning to hurt this historical site.

* * *

Outside, Ben, Dominic, and Ella are waiting.

"So where's Zoe today?" Ella asks the group.

"She'll catch up with us," says Ben. "She said she was eating lunch at home so she could wait for the mail. I guess she was getting a box from Scotland."

Once again confirming she left her heart—and maybe her brain—on a sheep farm across the Atlantic. I tell myself to relax. Re-acclimating takes time. But I hope the box doesn't have more haggis chips.

Ella must have been watching me because she leans over and whispers, "She'll be fine, Q. Born a Mainah, always a Mainah. Right? Isn't that what you told me?"

Well, that kind of makes me want to cry. I'm on the verge of tears much too much lately. I do not care for it. Focus.

Dominic also seems to sense that something's up with me. "What was that with the Lone Man?"

"Let's go to the beach and I'll tell you," I say. I always get my focus from looking at the ocean.

* * *

"So?" Dominic demands. "What did Lone Man show you on his phone?"

"Pictures of buildings—cafés from the olden days." It takes me a while to explain it all, but eventually I get across that Martin Candor seems to be the real deal when it comes to architecture, and we can cross him off our list once and for all.

At the end of the beach, we find Ms. Stillford sitting on a rock, staring out to sea. It strikes me how much more gray—and how much less blonde—her hair is than it was last summer. She seems unaware of us as we approach. One of her Birkenstock sandals is dangling off her foot as she leans back with the sun on her face.

She startles a little when I say, "Hi, Ms. Stillford!"

She points to a shallow reedy area between two sandbars. "Remember when that bed used to have decent clams? And we used to take pails out there?"

"That was fun," Ben says.

I stare out at the old clam bed like I'm watching myself seven years ago, wearing shorts and a canvas hat, bent over, digging in the wet sand for quahogs with Ben and Zoe.

"You and Zoe would have been six, Quinnie, and you seven, Ben." She shifts on the rock and goes silent for a couple seconds. "Such happy times."

The way she says it is so sad, like we don't have happy times anymore. I want to give her a big hug, but she's perched up on the rock. Instead, I lean against it. "We have lots more happy times to come, Ms. Stillford."

She shakes her head a little. "So much change. Too much change."

Ben tries in his way to lighten the mood. "Yeah, that Hubert restaurant is too weird, with its asparagus spoom and all."

Ms. Stillford laughs. "Oh, I don't know. The food is fine, I suppose. It just doesn't feel very Maiden Rock." She turns to me. "No need to tell your dad, Quinnie. I had to find out what it was like, but I won't be going a second time."

"Did you have the lobster with the beam of light?" Ella asks.

"Sounds like you kids have been reading the menu. No, I had sunchoke, oyster, and eggplant involtini with celery-infused cream. It was actually very tasty but too expensive. The place has an ambiance, though, I'll grant it that." She laughs again. "The day I was there, so was that woman with the dog, and she was giving the waiter *what for* because the salad plates weren't cold enough. She poked her finger in his face and demanded the plates be five degrees cooler!"

Ms. Stillford gets down off the rock and looks from the ocean to the row of beach houses. "I never thought I'd say this, but I don't want to see America. Not if it means spending the next year away from Maiden Rock."

Ella rushes over and hugs her. "You don't have to! Just stay here."

"Owen doesn't really want to go either," Ms. Stillford admits.

This cracks my heart wide open. Ella has her arms around Ms. Stillford's shoulders, so I go for her waist. I'm squeezing her with my face pressed against her back, and the next thing I know Ben is standing by us joining the hug-in. Not to be left out, Dominic piles on.

From deep within our little huddle, I hear Ms. Stillford say, "I love you kids."

24

Later that afternoon, I'm back at home, and I hear
Mom on the phone in her office. She's talking to
Detective John Dobson in Rook River. He used to
be *Officer* Dobson, and he'd really get on her nerves,
but then he backed her up in a huge way when Ms.
Stillford went missing, and they became good friends.
He's the one who loaned her the plainclothesman to
watch the café at night after the spice incident.

"I understand, John, there are staffing shortages
across the state. And I sure do appreciate what you've
been able to do for us . . . Yes, that's right, no activity
for five nights . . . It's all quiet . . . Well, okay then.
Thanks for the help."

Mom's chair squeaks like she's rocking in it and
thinking. Then she phones Dad. I stand very still.

"Gus, Dobson needs his man back . . . We've had
him out there drinking coffee in the bushes for five

nights . . . Oh, you're right about that. No one's getting through those new locks."

Dad seems to talk for a long time.

"I agree," Mom says. "Let's give it a rest for now. If we think we still have a problem later on, I'll go get a security camera and set it up."

As their conversation turns to commercial cleaning products, I resume walking out the door. I can't quite believe Mom's going to stop the live surveillance on Gusty's. Sure, I get that Dobson can't provide it anymore, and sure, I get that she thinks the new locks are going to be secure, and sure, maybe the perpetrator hasn't shown up for the last five nights, but what does that really tell us?

It doesn't tell us we are ironclad safe. It's playing the odds. The perp may have been watching the plainclothesman while he sat in the bushes. Maybe the minute our saboteur sees he has another chance, he'll take it. Plus, who knows how good he is at lock picking? For some criminals, there's no lock they can't pick.

When I get to Dominic's room I ask, "Hey, have you packed your video camera yet?"

"Yep. I couldn't even tell you what box it's in. Why?"

"We have a mission."

"What is it?" Dominic asks.

"The Rook River sheriff's office is pulling its surveillance officer, and my mom isn't going to replace him because she thinks the locks are good enough."

Zoe walks in at that moment. I texted her to meet us just to be sure she wasn't moping in her room. "What's up?"

Dominic doesn't notice her. He's already gone into planning mode. "We could post two people inside, two outside in the back, and one out front, ready to record with their phones. And where would we put the camera? If I can find it, that is."

"The back door, of course. That's the point of entry," I say.

Zoe waves her hands. "Oh no. No more break-ins or stakeouts or sting operations."

"It's not a break-in, Zoe," I tell her. "It's my family's café."

Dominic, trying to stay above the fray, starts assigning tasks. "Ben and I can be in back with the camera. Ella and Quinnie can be inside. And Zoe, you can be out front."

"Sorry, guys. No can do. The only way I'll be out front is if I'm across the street and upstairs in my room."

"That's good enough," says Dominic.

I know I should let the point go, but: "We're trying to catch the person breaking in. And not even physically catch them." I can hear my mother's voice if she stumbled upon this conversation. I reiterate the safety of what we're doing. "Just get footage of them breaking in."

"What if they try to set the place on fire?" Zoe asks. "And some of you are inside?"

I'm miffed at her for even imagining it. "Don't say that."

"I'm just saying," Zoe says.

"And I'm saying, don't say it," I snap.

Zoe looks shocked. For a second, I think she's going to tear up.

Dominic just stares at me.

"What?" I say. "Thoughts are powerful. That's all."

Without saying a word, Zoe turns and walks away.

"Zoe!" I call out. "Come on!"

Dominic's still looking at me.

I ask him, "You gonna find that camera?"

. . .

As I head back to my house, I try to forget about Zoe storming off. Sharing the new plan with Ben and Ella is just more important right now. When I reach my front porch, Mrs. Billingsley is coming out with her big bag over one arm and Groucho in the other. In her hand is a key. I wait for her to come down before heading up, but she lingers.

"Hello, young lady."

"Hi." I reach out to pet Groucho, who wriggles happily.

"Go ahead, might as well," Mrs. Billingsley says and kisses Groucho on the top of his head. "He's just impossible to resist."

I give the little guy's head a good scratching, and he stretches his neck for more.

"Okay. That's enough," Mrs. Billingsley says. "We have to go."

Groucho keeps his eyes on me and wags his tail as Mrs. Billingsley gets into the car and slams the door. Inside the car, the dog jumps up and down like a ping-pong ball. He's cute, but he's a weird one.

Mom's in her office, standing at her real estate desk and wearing her sheriff's uniform, but her top button is unbuttoned and her shoulders are sagging a bit.

"What did Mrs. Groucho want?" I ask her.

"The toilet has a bad smell. The bathroom faucet drips. The freezer doesn't make the ice hard enough. And now she's lost her dratted key." Mom shakes her head. "I had to charge her the full fifty dollars for a replacement. I mean, what am I supposed to do? It's in the rental contract." She turns and looks at me like she's just realized I'm there, even though we've been having a conversation. "How's packing going for the Moldartos?"

I don't exactly roll my eyes. I should be used to this by now. She always knows where I am and where I've been. She has the greatest spy network in the world. "They're almost done."

"Here, let me give you a new Gusty's key." She opens a paper envelope and shakes out a bigger, heftier key than we had before. "We had the café locks changed last night. Would've liked it done even sooner, but we had to do a special order to get the really strong stuff."

I turn the key over in my hand. It has real weight to it, as if it's taking the threat seriously. That doesn't change the fact that someone with ill intent might put our new locks to the test.

* * *

At eleven thirty that night, Dominic and Ben are by the back entrance of Gusty's, hidden behind some crates and barrels, armed with their phones and Dominic's camera, prepared to record anything that happens. Zoe is by her bedroom window, watching—I hope. Maiden Rock is partially overcast, with thunder rumbling in the distance, and for a second, I think Zoe might be the smart one.

Ella and I sneak into the café using my heavy new key. We don't turn on any lights, so Ella creates just a little bit of noise when she knocks over something metallic and shouts, "What the—?!" when it hits the floor.

I bump into a stack of dishes, almost sending them cascading to certain death. My heart races as I steady the tower of crockery. There's moisture hanging in the kitchen air from the steam cleaning that was done before lockup, and it starts to bead up on my forehead.

I feel my way to the counter, where moonlight coming through the front window reveals the chairs doing handstands on the tables. Zoe's house is dark across the street, but I see a flash of light in her window. Is she signaling me?

I text the team:

Me: *Zoe? That your light?*

Zoe: *Letting you know I'm here.*

I want to tell her to turn it back off so she doesn't scare off the saboteur. But instead I say:

Me: *Good. Lay low.*

Thankfully, I see the light snap off a few seconds later.

With that settled, I crouch behind the counter, in a space next to the ice bin. From there, I can peek up and look across the dining room or into the kitchen.

I call to Ella: "You set?"

"I'm in the pantry, behind a shelf of canned corn."

"Just don't knock it over."

"Fine, but can we make an espresso?"

I laugh. "Sure, I'll get right on that."

Our voices fade, and the quiet of the empty restaurant surrounds us. I hear a click–click–click and hold my breath. It continues: click–click–click. I turn my head, homing in on the direction of the sound. It's coming from ten or so feet from me, at the end of the counter near the wall. Click–click–click.

I realize the source and relax. The water reservoir in the big fancy espresso maker.

I sit down again and tuck my feet tightly under me, shivering. This place that's so familiar to me suddenly seems foreign and spooky. The time on my phone says eleven forty-seven p.m. It's going to be a long, stressful night if I keep freaking out over every little sound.

After an hour and a half of waiting, my legs are

cramping so bad that I need to stretch them out. I consider getting a Moxie out of the cooler when my phone lights up:

Zoe: *!!!!!!!!!! Man sneaking around café!*

Ben: *Where?*

Zoe: *On the side!!!!!!*

Ben: *Which side?*

Zoe: *Right side!!!*

Dominic: *Your right or our right?*

Zoe: *NOW!!!*

Me: *Do you see him?*

All of a sudden, I feel like Ella and I are sitting ducks, and our stakeout doesn't seem like such a good idea anymore.

Ben: *Got eyes. They're looking in the back windows. Can't tell who. D's trying to get footage.*

Ben: *He's at back door now. Fiddling with the doorknob! Dom still filming. Holy*

My fingers fly.

Me: *Wwhus hai?*

A crashing thud at the back door makes me jump. I don't know whether to sprint out there or hide where I am. I consider crouching by Ella so we're together. But before I can decide, Ella comes running to me, grabs my arm, and pulls me toward the front door.

"Come on," she yells. "Let's get out of here!"

We rush to the front and fumble to turn back the dead bolt, then push each other through the door. Ella yells, "Hey!" She's pointing up Mile Stretch Road, in the direction of Hubert's. A flash of lightning down the road reveals a dark figure in the distance. Ben's behind it, giving chase, but he's a long way's away.

"Ben, stop!" Ella yells. "He could get himself killed."

The rain reaches the Gusty's lot, running down our faces. Ella's Midnight Garden Azure eye shadow is all over her cheeks.

"Hey!" Dominic runs up to us. "Which way did they go?"

Ella points to the road, and Dominic starts in that direction. I grab his sleeve. "No, it's not safe! What happened?"

He yanks himself away. "We knocked over some crates, and that scared the man in black, and he bolted, and Ben yelled, 'Stop!' and busted it after him, and now Ben's out there alone with that guy."

I can tell there's no stopping him. Dominic's gone by the time the next flash of lighting reveals the now-empty road. I start pacing. This is way out of control. My first reaction is to call my mom—I mean, Ben and Dominic could be in real trouble. Then Ella goes rogue and races off after the guys.

"Wait!" I'm torn between joining the chase and closing up the café, which has its front door swinging open. This is crazy.

Me: *Come get the key and lock up the café so I can go with them.*

Zoe: *Now?*

Me: *YES NOW*

Zoe: *My parents might wake up.*

Me: *They won't.*

Zoe: *They might.*

Me: *Don't be lame. Come on.*

Zoe: *Not if you're going to be like that.*

Me: *NEVER MIND*

By the time we finish arguing, I look up and see Dominic, Ben, and Ella walking back toward me. I wave them into the dark café and lock the door behind us. We need to know who this guy is.

25

We hustle through the café and look out the back door.

"We were right there," Ben says, "hiding behind those barrels."

"I started recording, and he came up here to the back door," Dominic adds.

"What did he look like?" I ask.

"Average, I guess," Dominic says. "No way to really tell. Black pants, black shoes, black hoodie, black face mask—like a ski mask, or like a bank robber."

"When we moved to get better footage, the crates tumbled down and hit the bins, and he was off like a bullet," Ben says. "It took me a few seconds to get my big feet out of the tangle of bins, and he had too much of a head start. I lost him down the convent driveway."

"So he didn't run to Hubert's?" I ask. I realize I'd been assuming it was Slick.

"Nope."

I know it's useless to do much more tonight. The good thing is that we kept the perp from doing more damage. Ella starts wiping the wet footprints up in the café. The guys stack the crates in place out back. As the rain pours down, I survey the area outside the back door. It could still be Slick, but if it's not, we'll just keep moving down the list.

* * *

By the time dawn breaks and the sun slices through the remaining clouds of last night's storm, I haven't slept a wink. Not since I crawled into bed at three fifteen. My soaked clothes are in a pile in the corner.

We've agreed to meet at Gusty's at eight, and after that, we're going to the carriage house, where we hope Ms. Stillford stays in her living room long enough for us to decide what to do about the man in black.

I've watched and re-watched Dominic's footage, but it's useless because of the dark night and the rain. Just when the figure becomes visible, the camera takes a crazy roll and falls to the ground. I go back and forth over whether I should show Mom the video or tell her what we saw. I know she'll just be frustrated—I mean *really* frustrated, because the chance that the man in black will try another nighttime trip to Gusty's after hearing Ben yell at him is like . . . zero.

So, we may have stopped another attack on Gusty's. On the other hand, we may have wrecked our chance at catching the culprit.

And then there is Zoe. She's gone silent. I know. I know. I have to face this. I have to apologize—which I really *shouldn't* have to do, but I will, because lifetime friendships are sacred. And *she* really should have come down and helped me—but yes, fine, she is still re-acclimating.

It's five seventeen a.m. when I take a deep breath and text her.

Me: *Are you there?*

Zoe: *I am now.*

Me: *Are you coming to breakfast?*

Zoe: *I don't think so.*

I knew it. This is going to be bad. This is an invitation to ask what's wrong. I get that I'm being stupid by asking, instead of just coming out and apologizing, but I do it anyway.

Me: *Why not?*

Zoe: *Why do you think?*

What am I supposed to say? That I called her lame? Asked her to leave the house in the middle of the night? What?

Me: *Asking you to come out in the rain?*

Zoe: *Really? That's your best guess?*

I'm not getting out of this easily. I begin to type, *I'm sorry*, but wait—why, again, am I apologizing? I add: *I'm sorry if you don't like helping save my dad's café.*

Still, before I press Send, I reconsider.

Me: *I'm sorry if I snapped at you. I'm sorry if you miss Scotland. I'm sorry if you don't like investigating.*

She replies at the speed of light.

Zoe: *I don't care if you bark at me! I do miss Scotland. But no one else cares about Scotland. No one wants to eat my treats. No one wants to hear what I've been doing on a farm for two years. No one wants to learn a beautiful dance and listen to beautiful ancient music. It's not JUST sheep, you know. The culture and history are amazing.*

Now I'm really feeling like a jerk.

Me: *I'm sorry, Zoe. That sucks.*

* * *

Zoe still doesn't come to breakfast, but I'm a little too weary to give the situation any more energy right now.

Mom is standing at the café counter in her real-estate clothes—pants, blouse, blazer—and draining a cup of coffee. Her briefcase lies open on the seat of the stool next to her. Several pictures of houses lie atop it. She's obviously waiting for a house-hunting client.

Owen Loney blends into the background in his usual spot, nursing a mug of coffee. Clooney's in full order-taking swing. The toddler mom and dad are wiping Cream of Wheat out of their kid's hair at a table by the wall.

"Look," Dominic leans over and whispers to me. "That dad's wearing black. Black shoes, black jeans, black T-shirt."

I grip his arm. "Does he look like the guy from last night?"

Ben, who's been seated on the other side of Dominic, says, "No way, too tall."

Dominic leans back. "You're right. Too tall."

The cinnamon bun in front of me distracts me for a moment. I use my fingers to separate the sweet, warm stretches of sticky goo trailing between the plate and my mouth.

"Incoming," Ben says.

We all turn to the door. Martin Candor walks in and looks around. When he locates Mom, his face brightens. "Margaret, good to see you."

They take seats at a table and pore over listing sheets. She tells him about taxes, mortgage interest rates, availability. He's giddy like a kid.

Dominic says, "You know"—he strokes his chin and studies Candor critically—"he's about the right size."

"Ha ha," I say. "Moving on."

26

Later that morning, we slog through boxes at the carriage house. Ms. Stillford tells us to keep going without her as she leaves in her old Volvo for the yarn shop in Rook River. Ella and I start pulling old *Down East* magazines out of a box, and the guys slide torn and bent cardboard boxes down from the rafters.

"Where's Zoe?" Ella asks me.

"She's at home, I think."

Ella flips through a magazine.

I add, "She still misses Scotland, and she's bummed no one will dance with her or listen to ancient Scottish folk music or whatever." I feel Ella's gaze on me. "I'm not being mean. She's having a super hard time. And I don't know what to do. I have a major mess on my hands with the café and no time to Scottish-dance."

Usually, Ella would make a sassy New Yorker quip at a time like this, but I can tell she's not going to. "Quinnie, let's concentrate on Gusty's and making sure your family business is safe. I understand how she feels, and we'll listen to lutes and bagpipes soon. *I'll* tell her that, if it helps. You have a lot going on."

"You'll tell her that?"

"I will. In my own way."

I blink back tears. Ella's an amazing friend . . . and also, Ella is right. I need to maintain my focus. Now if only I can continue to pay as little attention as possible to Dominic leaving in six days.

Ben and Dominic, meanwhile, are reassessing our suspects by size. "Yeah. Could have been either of the Lewises," Ben says.

"What about the health inspector?" Dominic asks. "If he's crooked, like you think, it could have been him. Maybe he's in really deep."

Ella says, "Monroe Spalding says, 'Sometimes they're in so deep they don't even make a shadow.'"

"Who's Monroe Spalding again?" Zoe asks from the driveway. Her hair is clean and up in a bouncy ponytail. Her clothes look fresh. She's seems much better than when I texted with her this morning. It looks like Ella's going to get her chance to make good on her promise.

"He's the detective in my dad's crime novels," Ella says. "He knows his stuff."

When Zoe gets close enough to me, I hesitate a second to see if a hug is welcome, then give her a big one. She smiles and hugs me back, although I'd have to describe it as weak.

"So I suppose"—Zoe digs in her pocket—"he would think this is valuable evidence?" She takes out her phone and shows us a picture of a dark figure sneaking across the street toward the café.

"That's him!" Dominic and Ben shout at the same time.

We crowd around her to study the shot. A blurry black figure is taking a stride—right foot forward— across the street. There is little clarity, but even from the blur, you can still get a sense of size and direction.

"Hey, from Zoe's window, it looks like he came from up the road," Ella says.

"Or from the beach," I say.

"Well, he ran back that same way when he left."

"I wonder if we could figure out exactly how tall he is from this," I tell the group. "Like by comparing him to something else in the picture? Then we could compare that height to the suspects?"

"Easy peasy," says Dominic.

"Yeah, no problem," says Ben. He takes the phone and enlarges the image with his fingers. "I'm sure there's something in here we can use, right, Dom?"

We're finally getting this under control. It's morphed from spot observations to a real investigation with a photo crime lab and everything.

Ella says, "So who's on the suspect list right now?"

I say, "Hubert, Slick, the inspector—"

Dominic adds, "Toddler Mom, Toddler Dad, Mrs. Lewis, and Mr. Lewis."

* * *

Zoe's photo launches us on a mission to get pictures of all the remaining suspects, so we can keep track of their heights instead of going back and forth about them. After that, we'll compare them to the figure in Zoe's picture. We're lucky that so many of them congregate at Gusty's. I can even go in and measure the height of the counter or a table for reference during the afternoon lull.

After we've snapped a few photos and made a few comparisons, we realize pretty quickly that we should compare shape as well as height. For example, it's clear that Hubert wasn't the man in black because of the width of Hubert's shoulders and length of his legs. I had no idea until we started this project how different people are from the waist to the floor. You can be the same height as someone else and have longer legs by a lot.

We can't add the inspector's height to our spreadsheet, because he hasn't been back in town since we started, and the picture we have of him with Slick by the kitchen door is useless. He has one foot downhill and he's slouching. But we have plenty of pictures of Slick. Ella took a great one in front of Restaurant Hubert, where he and Hubert are talking to Mrs. Billingsley. She's shaking her finger in Hubert's face, like she's telling him what's wrong with his food, and he's clammed up and looking annoyed. Ella said she almost spat out laughing while it was happening, nearly giving away her hiding spot in the bushes.

"She was telling him things like, 'The beets have no taste,'" Ella says. "And 'This place will never be five stars if the pickled radishes burn the roof of people's mouths!'"

We're in my room that night, studying the picture in order to compare Slick and Hubert.

"At least my dad humors her," I say.

"Maybe your dad ought to give her that sour look that Hubert's giving her."

"That lady can't leave soon enough for me," I say. "Although, if she left Groucho behind, that would be cool."

27

At seven the next morning, I wake up feeling like things are coming into focus and life is getting under control. Zoe seems to have calmed down, we thwarted the most recent assault on the café, and we have a solid investigation underway. Soon we'll be able to identify the culprit and turn over credible evidence to Mom—hopefully before the end of the competition. That's going to wrap up in the next couple of days, and maybe then Dad can relax a little.

Of course, there is the little problem that Dominic is leaving in *five days* now, and he and I haven't really talked about it. My gut tells me we're supposed to talk about it. We don't just wait until he gets in the car and wave good-bye to each other, do we? How stupid would that be?

So why am I not saying anything? Why is he not

saying anything? I guess I don't know what to say. Maybe it just comes to you. Or maybe you have to make it come to you.

But what if the wrong thing comes to you? How stupid is this? I'm getting out of this bed and going over there right now and saying something—whatever comes to me. I kick off the covers.

* * *

I dart and weave around the Moldartos' half-filled boxes on my way to the stairs. His bedroom door is open. I smell him before I see him. It's the smell of soap and wet hair. I pause for a second. "You dressed?"

"Hey. Come on in."

I stick my head through the doorway and look around the room. Dominic's wearing jeans and his T with the omega symbol on the front. There is no getting around it—the shirt is a rag, and it's too small for him. He's grown a foot in the past year, easily, and I haven't seen that shirt for months.

"Might be time to retire the omega T."

Dominic looks down at his taller, skinnier self. "Yeah. I'm throwing out a bunch of stuff. I thought I'd try it on for old times' sake. Too small, huh?"

"Not for me."

He smiles, peels it off, and tosses it to me. "Done. Want any of my other junk?" He reaches for a white T-shirt with *Gusty's of Maiden Rock—Home of Gusty Burgers and Lobster Fries* on the front and pulls it over his head. A second after that, on goes his signature slouchy hat, right on top of wet hair. This is so him.

Dominic digs more clothes out of his closet and throws them in a box. When I see what he's tossing, I realize how much of a Mainah he's become: L.L.Bean fleece, storm jacket, boat shoes, plaid shirts. He drifts to the shelf where his Funko Pop collection is displayed. After studying it like a chess board, he carefully selects one.

He clears his throat. "Quinnette Boyd, please rise."

I stand, brush some hair out of my face, and hold my hand out, palm up.

"I present you with my Sherlock Holmes Funko Pop, in recognition of your service to Maiden Rock, Maine." He hands it to me like an Oscar.

"I'd like to thank the Academy—"

"Uh, excuse me." He snatches it back out of my hand. "*Who* exactly are you thanking for this classic collectable?"

I straighten up and put my hand out again. "Okay. Okay. I'd like to thank Dominic Moldarto, and I accept this passing of the geek baton. How was that?"

"Much better."

"But it's too soon."

"Are you kidding? I'm not halfway done." He looks under his bed and pulls out a dark blue Vans shoe. "Do you see the other one of these?"

I get up and start digging around in the bottom of the closet. It's not there. I look under piles of clothes and boxes. Not there. "Nope. I don't see it."

"Man, I'm going to miss that shoe."

He's standing there with one shoe in his hand and his wet hair curling under his cap, smelling like a shower, being so completely who he is, and I know, like I know that Moxie runs in my veins, that I am going to miss him with my whole heart.

"I don't want you to pack," I say, instead of *I don't want you to leave.*

"I don't want to pack, either," he says, instead of *I don't want to leave.* "Maybe we should go eat breakfast."

"Yeah. I think so."

"We have to catch this guy soon," he says, instead of *I'm leaving soon.*

"Yep, pretty soon." Neither of us wants to put a number on it, even though we both know it's five days until Dominic's gone.

We have our arms around each other's waist as we walk down the stairs. We let go as we walk into the bright morning light. I'm calling this progress.

* * *

When Dominic and I reach the café, we spot Ella's dad standing by his car and talking to Martin Candor. They're in a mildly animated conversation.

"I didn't know they knew each other," I say.

"Maybe they don't," Dominic replies. "Maybe they're just saying 'Hey' and talking about the weather."

Ella walks up to us. "What? What are you looking at?"

"Your dad is talking to Martin. Does he know him?" I ask.

"No, I don't think so."

We watch them walk through the café door— Martin Candor, followed by Mr. Philpotts.

"Far be it from me to point out that he could be the Secret Diner," Dominic says. "That's another issue I'm still curious about."

"Why do you say that?" I ask. "He's been checked out. He's a real architect."

"Didn't Ella's dad set the contest up with the

Rook River paper?" Dominic asks. "Isn't he the one who convinced the Secret Diner to visit?"

Ella shrugs like she can't deny it but isn't convinced by Dominic's theory either.

Mom waves to Martin. "Martin, you ready for a second look at a few houses?"

"Hi, Margaret. I sure am."

He joins her at the counter, and she starts talking intently about financing, possession dates, and recent updates to wiring and plumbing.

Before we can decide whether that settles the question of Martin's secret identity, if he is neither a crook nor a critic, Clooney reaches our table. "What's it going to be? Special is bacon waffles with blueberry syrup."

We all order the special, except Ben, who arrives late and orders an egg-and-bacon sandwich, a cinnamon bun, and two milks. I don't know where he puts it.

"I've been thinking," Ben says through bites of bun, "about how this conspiracy might be working."

"Go ahead," I say.

"Well, suppose Hubert's at the head, because he wants to get all the business in town. He has a loyal guy in Slick. He pays Slick to take care of the logistics. Slick then hires the inspector to do the dirty work—flagging violations at Gusty's, breaking into the café."

"So, one to ten, how much do we think the guy we saw the other night was the inspector?" Dominic asks.

I have to think hard about this. "At this point in time, based on what we know, I'm giving it an eight," I say. "Because he would know exactly what to mess with at Gusty's to make the café most vulnerable."

"We need another picture of that guy," says Ben.

"Well, then," Dominic says, "today's your lucky day."

28

As if he heard we were looking for him, the inspector strides into the café like he's expecting to be saluted.

"He's so pompous," Ella whispers.

"He's so the right size," Dominic says.

Clooney rushes to the kitchen, and a few seconds later Dad comes out, wiping his hands on a white towel. He and the inspector meet by the counter. I can tell Dad is trying to get him to walk into the kitchen, away from the diners, but the inspector's not moving.

"I'm going to stand near him," Dominic says, getting up. "Ella, you get our pictures."

I slip to a seat at the counter, darting my eyes between my friends, the inspector, and Dad. But before Ella can snap a pic, Dad and the inspector head back into the kitchen. It's five long minutes before they step back out.

"Here's your re-inspection report." The man unclips a sheet of paper and hands it to Dad.

Dad's eyes race over the front of it, then he flips it over and looks at the back. I watch his eyeballs go to the bottom of the back page. His shoulders relax.

"Thanks," he says.

"It's looking okay—for now," the inspector says. "You probably want it to stay that way."

Dad tilts his head slowly, as if he's trying to figure out if there's some special meaning to what the inspector just said. He must conclude there's not, because he breaks into a smile and sticks his hand out to the man. "We sure do," he says.

The inspector shakes Dad's hand but doesn't smile back. "Right, then."

"Cup of coffee?" Dad asks him. "Latte? Americano? On the house?"

Now the man smiles. "You wouldn't be trying to induce me to keep giving you good inspections, would you?"

Dad laughs.

"Because that would take a lot more than a latte," the inspector continues. He laughs loud and heartily slaps Dad on the back.

Once the inspector is gone, Dad wipes his hands on the towel again, picks up a coffeepot, and approaches Owen Loney in his seat at the counter's end. "More coffee, Owen?"

Owen pushes his mug toward Dad. "What did that fella want?"

"He said the place is looking okay, and I *probably want to keep it that way*," says Dad.

"Sure you would," says Owen.

"I don't think that's what he meant," says Dad.

"Maybe he wants . . ." Owen rubs two weathered fingertips together like he means money.

"Damn right that's what he wants, and I'll tell you, that's not gonna happen. He's messing with Gustav Boyd the Third."

Yes, Dad! I'm about to jump into their conversation when a nasally voice starts talking loudly into a cell phone. I turn to see Mrs. Billingsley and Groucho at a nearby table. She's bossing around someone on the other end.

"Just tell me what you're going to do about it, because that was a very expensive dress, and it's worthless to me without the belt. Honestly, a person brings one dress to a dry cleaner, and you people can't keep track of the matching belt . . . yes, *very* expensive . . ."

Thankfully, Mr. Philpotts comes up to the counter, blocking out the painful conversation.

"Gus, my fine man," Mr. Philpotts says, "I'll have one of your tasty double espressos."

"Coming up," says Dad.

A hissing cloud of steam appears as Dad manipulates the levers on the ornate Italian coffee maker. Dense black liquid streams into a tempered glass, and Dad places it in front of Ella's dad with a flourish. "Here you go."

Mr. Philpotts raises the espresso to his nose and savors it with his eyes closed. "Gus, you have become a master barista."

Dad beams and wipes the counter with that towel he cannot seem to put down.

"You know"—Mr. Philpotts leans over his espresso—"with fine coffee like this, it's no doubt you're holding down a small lead in the Secret Diner competition."

Dad, Dominic, Owen Loney, and I all look at him.

Dad says, "You know this? For sure?"

Ella's dad sips his double espresso and says, "I have my sources."

I look over at our table, where Ella and Ben are talking with their heads close together. Then I check out a few other tables. The Lewises are not at the café. The toddler parents are catching flying strawberries from their kid's small, sticky hands. The sisters are finishing plates of pancakes. And Mrs. Billingsley is still listening to her phone, making a nasty face. At the same time, she's feeding bits of cinnamon bun to Groucho.

I'm tempted to tell Dad our latest hunch about the conspiracy, but I know he will be on the phone to Mom soon to tell her about the inspector's not-so-subtle request for a payoff. But before I can say anything to Dad *or* Dad can call Mom, Mrs. Billingsley starts telling Dad that her waffle is cold and that they should be served within one minute of being taken out of the iron. So I begin revisiting all the scenes at Restaurant Hubert: seeing the inspector outside, being in the kitchen and watching Hubert scratch his belly, witnessing the sick man being taken away, Ben and Dominic's shots of Slick and the inspector, the time Ella snapped a photo of Slick and Hubert being chewed out by Mrs. Billingsley in front of the restaurant.

By the time I reach that last one, Mrs. Billingsley is telling Clooney, at the top of her lungs, that her table isn't clean. Other diners look at her, then check their own tables. I wonder if anyone in the café at this moment is the Secret Diner. Could something like this affect the competition?

Suddenly, the craziest idea strikes me. Is Mrs. Billingsley part of the conspiracy? Is she in here all the time, complaining, for the purpose of driving people away? I check myself. That's pretty flimsy, since she's driving people away from Hubert's too. But still—groan—I have *too many* suspects. Maybe it's a good time to tell Mom everything I know.

29

Before I talk to Mom, I have to wait until she's out of real-estate wonderland, where she's concentrating on making a sale. If Martin Candor decides to buy a house, this could take all day—and we don't have all day. The contest ends tomorrow, lucky day seventeen, and the winner will be announced at a ceremony at Gusty's at one o'clock. (Dad won a coin toss for the location.) If the man in black is going to strike again, he's going to do it before the big announcement— probably tonight!

Dominic and I decide to position ourselves at my house. That way, we can talk to my mom as soon as she's home. Ella and Ben are going on a roaming patrol, back and forth on Mile Stretch Road between Gusty's and Hubert's, looking for suspicious behavior.

I've printed out our photos and spreadsheets and laid them on the dining room table. While we wait for my mom, Dominic compares the height of the man in black to the height of the trash bin in Zoe's yard. Based on the trash bin, he estimates the guy to be five feet, eight or nine inches tall. I suggest the extra inch because he's leaning over as he runs. We organize the facts and figures and try to reach some conclusions based upon motive, means, and opportunity.

Finally, at two p.m., we hear Mom come in the front door. It's immediately clear that Dad shared the news about the inspector, because she's on the phone, asking to speak to the state director of health inspection. We listen as she walks down the hall into the kitchen.

"Yes, this is Sheriff Margaret Boyd in Maiden Rock . . . yes. I'd like to get some background information on the inspector you've been sending to this town . . . Yes, I have a signed form with the name . . . Hold on."

Mom sticks her head into the dining room, still holding the phone to her ear. She looks at us and the mess on the table and raises her eyebrows as if to say, what's all this? Then she puts her finger to her lips and walks back to her office.

We wait another twenty minutes while she makes more phone calls. I can't tell what she's saying, but the strident tone of her voice tells me the inspector is under her microscope. I've paced around the table twenty times and sat in a few different chairs. Dominic has drifted to the back porch and back. We finally decide to hang on the front steps. This way, we'll be closer when she gets off the phone. I check the clock in the hallway. It's three thirty p.m. Time is wasting.

From our seat on the front steps, we get a good show. Summer people walk up and down the road, thrilled with themselves for discovering Maiden Rock. Ben's uncle John drives up to the intersection in his pickup and gives us the two-finger wave from his steering wheel before he turns toward Gusty's. Mrs. Billingsley cruises up to a stop sign, taking a right turn out of town. She doesn't look at us, but Groucho's bouncing in her lap, yipping hello.

Dominic asks me, "Do you think we could get a play date with that dog?"

Before I can answer, the door opens and Mom says, "What's going on out here? And what's that stuff on the dining room table?"

I jump up and say, "We have to show you something."

＊ ＊ ＊

"Sit here." I pull out a chair for Mom.

Her eyes are searching the tabletop as she sits, taking it all in.

"We want to tell you everything we know."

She closes her eyes for a second, takes a deep breath, and says, "Okay, shoot."

"We already know Hubert and Slick could have motive," I tell her. "And Ben and Dominic even saw Slick give the inspector an envelope after the bad inspection at Gusty's. *And* the inspector said some things to Dad that sounded like he was asking for a payoff in exchange for good inspections."

"That could mean he's extorting money from both of them or double-crossing Willy and Hubert," Dominic says.

I broach the larger theory. "Hubert, Willy, and the inspector may be part of a conspiracy to put Gusty's out of business."

"Okay," Mom says. "I understand your suspicions about Hubert and Willy and even the inspector."

Dominic adds, "And the Toddler Dad. He's about the same size as the man in black."

"He has *no motive*," Mom says. "Hold on. What man in black?"

Dominic and I fall mute. I didn't expect it to come out this way.

I reach for Zoe's photograph and the spreadsheet with our suspect-height comparisons.

"Wait a minute. Wait a minute. Where and when was this photo taken?" Mom wants to know.

I say this very carefully, not mentioning more than I need to about my stakeout. "Zoe snapped it from her bedroom window, about 1:15 a.m."

"Did he go around the back of Gusty's?"

"Yes. And then ran out the other side and ran away."

Mom is thinking to herself, so I don't say anything else. I'm hoping Dominic doesn't either.

"I can't believe we had that fellow out there all those nights, and nothing. Then, the first night he's gone, bam! Well, we're going to need Detective Dobson again. I have to make a call."

But before she leaves the room, she turns toward me.

"And if Dobson's officers catch *you* out there tonight, there will be nothing I can do for you. So you've been warned. Get it?"

30

Obviously we're not running a stakeout tonight. Mom has it covered. I feel good about this, but I'm also at a loss. I need to be doing something to protect Gusty's too.

Everyone's antsy. Ben and Dominic insist they're going to keep a midnight eye on Restaurant Hubert. I make them promise not to go near Gusty's and get arrested by Mom's security patrol. Zoe wants no part of any of it, and she proposes a Scottish-music sleepover with me and Ella at my house. I try to steer the sleepover to Zoe's current house, so I can watch out the window, but Ella wants to have it at *her* house so we can do makeovers. Just around the time I'm ready to throw up my hands and say forget it, we settle on my place. Zoe is delighted. But first, Ella, Ben, Dominic, and I head to Gusty's to check out the preparations for the big day tomorrow.

Dad and Clooney are jumping around like water beads on a hot griddle. He's polishing the espresso machine and steam cleaning all the glassware at the same time she's cooking and serving. Clooney says she wishes they didn't have to serve breakfast tomorrow morning. She's thinking how nice it would be to start with the big-deal lunch—the last meal the Secret Diner will be judging. Dad agrees and keeps checking ingredients over and over.

Dad lets us kids wash the windows and straighten the lending library shelves, even though they don't need it. Mom is outside in plainclothes, talking to her team. Anyone can see that they're Dobson's men. They're not wearing uniforms but they have the look. And their car is a dull black muscle car with tinted windows. Dead giveaway. Dominic is drawn to it like a magnet, but a glare from Mom tells him to keep his distance.

* * *

The café is pretty full for dinner. There are some new faces, as well as some regulars. Dad says the Secret Diner must be here. Maybe. He could be at Hubert's instead. Either way, this Secret Diner has done a heck of a job remaining secret.

The sisters arrive and grab their favorite table. Martin Candor has shown up too, and the Lewises, and the toddler family. Soon, there are no free tables left over. Mrs. Billingsley arrives and looks around. When she doesn't see any open seating, she walks over to the sisters and stands by the nearest empty chair until they ask her if she wants to join them. She does.

My crew, minus Zoe—who's repacking some of her stuff before her family moves back to their normal house—grabs our table and watches everything and everyone.

I look out the windows. They sparkle. My eyes drift down to the floor, to be sure it's been thoroughly swept, and I see a corner that we missed.

"Hey, you guys. I'm going to get a dustpan and broom and clean that corner."

"Relax," Ella says. "It all looks great."

I get up and head for the back of the café anyway. "It'll just take a second."

The cleaning supplies are in a closet between the pantry and the back door. As I turn on the light near the closet, something shiny flashes at me from the floor. It's in front of the closed closet door, off to the side a little ways. A key.

I pick it up and flip it over in my palm. It looks like every other key in this town. Until we got the new heavy-duty café locks, Mom had all of the locks in her care—for the café, our house, and all the rental houses that she manages—made in the same style, with the same kind of brass key for each. This is one of the old models, which means the lock it goes with could be almost anywhere in Maiden Rock.

Clooney is busy in the kitchen, her arms flying like an octopus as she makes up plates and fills take-away boxes.

"Hey Clooney," I call to her. "Do you still have your old key to the café? Can I look at it?"

She doesn't look up from flipping burgers on the griddle. "Yep. Still got it. In my jacket pocket over there."

Clooney's key ring has four keys on it. I eliminate the one that matches my new café key. Then I compare the other three keys, one of which has to be Clooney's old café key, to the key I just found by the closet. It's weird, though—they're all the same kind of brass, but none of the ridges on Clooney's keys match the key from the floor.

Hmm. If my new finding isn't even an old café key, what's it for? Is this a clue? That's definitely what my gut says.

Dad hurries through the kitchen, and I call out to him. "Hey Dad, have you lost any of your keys?"

Despite having an armful of towels for the laundry pile, he gives it a second of thought. "Nope."

I walk back into the dining room, to our table, and hold the key from the floor up to the group. "I just found this by the back door."

As everyone reaches out to touch it, I realize I've broken a cardinal rule of investigating and put my stupid paws all over it. "Uh-oh. Fingerprints destroyed."

Then Dominic says something that boosts my spirits just a little: "By the back door, huh? The man in black was fiddling around at the back door."

"Yeah," Ben says, "but he didn't get in."

I sit up straight. "Yes, he did—the night of the spices, maybe earlier too. He could have dropped it without knowing it while he messed the spices up."

I don't even remember ordering, but somehow food is in front of us. I'm lost in an idea. It's not an old Gusty's key, but it's definitely a Maiden Rock key. No mistaking the locksmith's usual design. So the person who dropped it lives in Maiden Rock.

That rules out the inspector.

But even if the person didn't notice right away that they had lost their key, they would've asked Mom for a replacement after a while, right? Slick, Hubert—Mom didn't mention either of them requesting one. And she always complains about replacement keys.

Wait a minute. Wait. One. Minute. Mrs. Billingsley lost a key the other day.

I look up and across the room at Mrs. Billingsley, who's still sitting with the sisters. Take away the hat, and maybe she isn't as old as she looks. Take off the gloves, and maybe the hands aren't so old and wrinkly.

Could Mrs. Billingsley be the man in black?

Nah. Yeh. Nah. Yeh. Nah. Maybe?

I take out my phone and look at that picture of her, Hubert, and Slick. We decided Slick was about the same size as the man in black. And I've got to admit, she's about the same size as Slick.

After a quick look for Mom outside, I head to the kitchen. She's near the sink, cutting a piece of blueberry pie.

"Mom?"

"Quinnie?"

"I think I know."

She takes a bite and swallows. "Know what?"

"The man in black, the spices, the dishwasher—you know, all of it."

"Explain."

"I think it's Mrs. Billingsley."

She shakes her head.

"Listen. I've seen her talking to Hubert. Maybe they even know each other."

I'm prepared to show her the key next. I'm convinced it will open the door of Mrs. Billingsley's rental.

"You are right about that, Quinnette," Mom says. "She's knows Hubert."

"What? What do you know?"

Mom continues: "*I know* that she's his mother."

"His mother?! How long have you had info like that?" I try not to sound accusatory.

"I sold him both the lobster pound and the farm, and her name was on the loan papers. She co-signed."

"Why didn't you tell anyone?"

"Because I had an email correspondence with her, and she asked me not to," Mom says. "She wanted Hubert to succeed on his own." Then she mutters, "But best I can tell, she pushes him really hard."

"But she could be helping him in criminal ways, right? I mean she could really, *really* want him to succeed."

"I don't get that from her at all, Q. Sneaking around the café at night—she doesn't fit the profile."

Mom walks to the door to the dining room and beckons me to come. "Look at her, Quinnie."

The scene is almost hilarious. Mrs. Billingsley has Groucho on her lap, and he's catching the french fries that Sister Rosie is tossing at him. Each time he catches one, Mrs. Billingsley claps with her gloved hands.

The grooves on the key are digging into my palm, even through the plastic bag. I'm about to open my fingers and show the key to Mom, but my embarrassment about the smudged fingerprints stops me. Besides, she'd just take the key and tell me she'll deal with it herself.

31

I slip the key into my pocket and go back to our table. Clooney Wickham is there, taking the dessert orders from everyone.

"We got three pieces of blueberry pie left, plenty of whoopie pies, gingerbread with hot lemon sauce, and maple walnut ice cream."

We all order without delay.

I keep my eye on the sisters' table, where Mrs. Billingsley is still fussing over Groucho, but I notice that Mom has grabbed an open seat at the counter. She appears to be watching them too. *Yes.* She listens to me. She may not realize it, but she does.

"Guys," I tell my table, "I know who the man in black is." All of their heads turn to me. "It's Mrs. Billingsley."

Ben laughs. "Okay, that's a little crazy."

Dominic jumps on the idea. "Dang. Yeah. Think about it. She's never been to Maiden Rock until now. She's a loner. She's not interested in meeting anyone unless it gets her a seat at the table. She stirs up trouble. She might actually know Hubert."

I pull out my phone, type *Billingsley* in the search bar, and add *and Pivot*. My screen fills up with links instantly. I can't believe this. During the search when I found those clips of Hubert, none of this appeared.

There's a stream of articles about a Massachusetts company Mrs. Billingsley owned. It was exposed as having never paid its employees the retirement pensions it had promised them.

"Are you ready for this?" I hand my phone over to Ella, who reads the story I've pulled up and gasps. She hands it to Ben, who says, "Whoa." He hands it to Dominic, who nods his head.

"See?" I tell them. "She's been involved in some shady stuff. And she has the right height, the right build."

"But what's *her* motivation?" Ella asks.

"She's his mother."

"*Whaa?* No! Seriously!?" Ben slaps his hand on the table.

I scroll through more pages of Pivot and Billingsley, and it doesn't take long. There's a picture of her with Hubert in happier times, in front of Shovela. I show it to the group.

Everyone's head turns back to Mrs. Billingsley. We sit and eat our whoopie pies so as not to raise suspicion, but as soon as we're done, we are out of there.

On the way to my house, we make a plan to sneak to Mrs. Billingsley's house after dark and check the key in her lock. If it opens the door—that's it, she's our man.

* * *

Waiting for my parents to go to sleep takes an eternity. Once sundown comes, the guys have to go home, despite their best efforts to hang with me, Ella, and Zoe, who has finished up what her mom calls *quality family time*. Dominic's dad actually walks over and says good night for him. Ben's uncle John calls him, and I can hear the command in his voice. That leaves me and Ella and Zoe on the back porch, where we're idling until we can find the right time to sneak up to beach house #16 and try the key.

"Kinda sucks to be back here, huh?" Ella says to Zoe.

Zoe's tucked up into a ball, hugging her knees. "Uh-huh."

"I sort of know," Ella says. "I mean, I moved to Maiden Rock from New York."

"Do you miss it?"

I'm listening intently for the answer.

"Not really," Ella says. "Not since Gusty's got an espresso maker, anyway."

"There are no guys here," Zoe says. "It didn't bother me when I was a little kid, but that sucks."

"There are lots of guys at Rook River High."

Then Zoe surprises me—she perks up and asks Ella to tell her about the tenth grade boys.

This is the most energized I've seen Zoe since she got back. With Dominic on my mind, I can't exactly relate, but it's good to see her looking forward to something.

By one a.m., my house has gone quiet and the town is still—except for the sound of the breaking waves. It's one of those smooth ocean nights. The moon shines on the glassy-topped swells and the waves tuck tight against the outcroppings, as if they're trying to be quiet too.

We sneak down my stairs and walk down the

beach toward #16. Our mission is solely to see if the key opens the front door. We pass five beach houses along the way. #11 is dark. No summer guest is occupying it yet. #12 has a faint light in an upstairs window. It may be the flickering of a TV. #13 is asleep, with towels drying on the porch rail. #14 is still boarded up. #15 is dark, but I know the Stevenses are inside. They're just sound asleep—I hope.

We walk between #15 and #16, ducking down and shushing each other. Since I did the walk-through with Mrs. Billingsley, I can assume she is sleeping in the big bedroom upstairs.

I take the key from my pocket and put my foot on the first wooden step to the door. It creaks. Ella and Zoe grab me. I don't know what would produce the least amount of ruckus—taking each step slowly or dashing up. I decide on a dash.

Creak. Crack. Snap!

Bark-bark-bark-bark.

Groucho is growling and howling and throwing himself at the window above us. For a split second, we're frozen. The light in the room overhead snaps on, shedding its glow on the steps below. We jump and dart like rabbits after gunfire—between the houses, up the beach, up our steps, onto the porch, and into our sleeping bags.

We don't talk. We're all breathing heavily. After about a half an hour of trying to calm ourselves down, our heartbeats have slowed, but we keep asking each other, "Are you awake?"

32

There are gulls cawing and people laughing on the beach when the morning light warms my face. My back aches from sleeping on the porch, but I struggle upright and jostle Ella and Zoe.

When I find my phone in my jeans and check it, there are three texts from Dominic.

Dominic: *Are you guys dead? It's the BIG DAY.*

Dominic: *There's a ton of buzz in town already.*

Dominic: *Hello? DID THE KEY FIT?*

My phone says it's 10:00. The final lunch of the contest happens at noon. I nudge Ella and Zoe and jump up and pull on my jeans and T. "We have to get going."

After rolling up our sleeping bags, we start pulling ourselves together in my room when there's a knock at the front door. I open it to find Beverly Billingsley, who is holding Groucho in a mini-chef outfit.

"I'm turning this in," she says. She holds out her gloved hand. "I thought I lost mine, but I found it. So here's the extra."

My mind is confused. What's she saying? I try to sound casual. "Oh, thanks. Where did you find it?"

"It was by my front door. It must have fallen out of my purse. So here is the duplicate that I had to pay for. I'd like my money back."

The fog in my head starts to clear. She's handing me the key. I must have dropped it last night.

I take it from her and fidget a bit. My fingers press the outside of my pocket. Yep, it's empty.

"I'll give it to my mom, and she'll call you or something."

"Okay, but I'm formally returning it as of now. So make sure and tell her."

She adjusts her bag on her shoulder. Groucho barks at me. He's never done that before.

* * *

We arrive at Gusty's at ten thirty. And, whoa! The crowd looks huge. Dominic and Ben are having a hard time hanging on to our table, so they're thrilled to have Zoe and Ella join them. I decide to take a look in the kitchen. Clooney Wickham is at the stove, on her tiptoes, stirring a giant pot with a long spoon. There's a second pot next to it. Steam rises from both of them, causing sweat beads on Clooney's face. Fish heads bob in the low simmer of the pots' broth. On the long prep counter, there are stacks of bowls waiting to be filled.

The tables are full—well, except for two of them. One has a tent on it that says *Rook River Advertiser and Guests*. The other says *Restaurant Hubert and Guests*. Sister Rosie and Sister Ethel have arrived in time for the festivities, sitting at a table with one open seat. I walk over to them to say hello.

"Oh, Quinnie, we're so excited," says Sister Rosie. She lowers her voice and leans toward me. "I'm sure Gusty's is going to win."

One of the chairs has been tipped against the table, and I put my hand on it.

"So sorry, dear! We're saving that for Beverly."

"Beverly?" I ask. I know what she said, but I'm surprised they're on such familiar terms.

"Yes, Mrs. Billingsley," Sister Rosie says. "You know, she's not as strange as she seems."

"She'll be here soon," Sister Ethel adds. "We told her we'd save a seat." Sister Ethel doesn't look as enthused as Sister Rosie.

I guess I would have expected Mrs. Billingsley to sit with her son, Hubert, unless they're keeping that all the way confidential. But when I look over to the Hubert table, it's starting to fill up with Willy and other people from the restaurant. Hubert himself hasn't arrived.

Dad dashes around with trays of lattes and espressos, giving out samples. At each table, he drops off the *Special of the Day* menu insert. In large blue script, it says *FISH HEAD SOUP with Pilot Crackers and a side of Garlicky Cole Slaw.*

I look at my phone. It's eleven ten. I head to my table and sit down. Everyone is chowing on Cheese Nips from a bowl in the center of our table. The whole room feels impatient, as if people might start pounding and chanting for the Secret Diner.

By eleven forty-five, Beverly Billingsley has arrived with Groucho, Ms. Stillford has joined Owen Loney at the counter, and Ella's dad has filled a seat at the table reserved for the Rook River paper.

Clooney is going around taking all the orders. At each table, she aggressively sells the special. After seeing the two pots in the kitchen, I can see why. We'll have a lot of soup to toss if people don't chow down. Although, I have to admit, the aroma coming from the kitchen is divine.

I go back to watching Beverly Billingsley. She and the sisters have already given their orders when I hear her begin to complain. "There isn't a Captain Mowatt's hot sauce here." Clooney turns to look at the table, but Sister Ethel rolls her eyes and motions for Clooney not to worry about it. "I'll get one," Sister Ethel says.

Sister Ethel strides to the counter, grabs the Captain Mowatt's, and puts it in front of Billingsley. Groucho stick his nose up to it, then jerks his head back and repeatedly licks his face. Clooney sees this and fumes.

In the midst of this, Hubert Pivot steps into Gusty's and locates his table. The toddler family is behind him. They search the room, see someone they know, and join them. Next come the Lewises. They squeeze in with people they don't know. The remaining seats at the Rook River newspaper table are taken by people I've never seen before. One of them has a stack of newspapers with him, as well as a large envelope.

Mom comes up to me, and I ask her, "Where's the Secret Diner?"

She says, "I guess if the Secret Diner were revealed here, that would be the end of the secret and the end of the column. All we get to know is the winner."

Everyone at my table grouses about this for a while. Here we've been doing all this guessing, and no one's going to tell us who it is. I notice that Billingsley is holding up the Captain Mowatt's bottle with two fingers. Screwing up her face, she says something about it being a disgusting, sticky mess. Knowing her, that probably means there was a dot of dried hot sauce on the bottle.

After the sisters don't give her complaints much attention, I notice Billingsley pick up her big bag—with Groucho in it—and hike it onto one shoulder. She uses her other hand to take the hot sauce bottle by its cap and then heads toward the kitchen door.

Clooney stops her and says, "You can't go in that kitchen—especially not with that dog."

Billingsley snorts, takes Groucho out of the bag, and plunks him in Clooney's arms, then disappears into the kitchen. Dad is across the dining room, talking to Mr. Philpotts, when he sees this go down. Mom's standing at the newspaper table, shaking hands, and the pair of police guys tries to signal her, with expressions that say, *Uh, Sheriff, is that lady supposed to go back there?*

By the time Clooney has handed the dog off to someone else and Dad has made his way around the tables, Beverly Billingsley is walking back out of the kitchen. She holds a towel, wiping off the Captain Mowatt's bottle she's apparently washed. "Sticky bottles," she says, shaking her head. "Now that's a health issue."

Once Billingsley has returned to her seat, I get up and walk to the kitchen door myself, since Mom is still schmoozing with the Rook River people. Slowly, carefully, I scan the shelves and countertops. Not sure what I'm looking for. But nothing looks missing—that I can tell.

Shaking off Billingsley's disruption, Clooney and Dad begin the grand soup service. They bring it out on large trays laden with hefty bowls. The aroma wafts from each bowl, causing patrons to stretch their necks and whisper *oohs* and *aahs*.

Someone calls out to Dad, "Have you added something new to the soup, Gus?"

"Nope. Same since the new menu."

Soon Clooney delivers the orders to our table. I sniff the contents of my bowl, which certainly smells like Gusty's Fish Head Soup, maybe a little more pungent than usual. Billingsley and the sisters get their orders next. Clooney moves on, and Rosie and Ethel dig in, but I notice that—although her spoon's in her bowl—Mrs. Billingsley's not eating. She's checking out the other diners.

I avert my eyes quickly so as not to connect with her. When I think she's not turned my way, I catch her raising a spoonful of soup to her mouth—and letting it drop back into the bowl. What the heck? If she doesn't want the special, why'd she even order it? She doesn't strike me as someone who feels any pressure to eat what everyone else eats.

I send a questioning glance toward Mom, who has taken a chair at the newspaper table. She gives me a *did you see that?* look. We both survey the room, but nothing else unusual seems to be happening. Mom motions to me to follow her to the kitchen, and she grabs Dad and Clooney on the way.

"What's up?" Dad asks.

Mom says, "Quinnie and I thought we saw Mrs. Billingsley . . ." She pauses as if she's at a loss for how to describe what I know we were both thinking.

"Pretending to eat the fish soup," I say.

"She's a dumb cluck," says Clooney.

"What are you talking about?" Dad asks. Looking through the kitchen doorway, he checks back on the dining room.

We all do. We see her do it. She lifts the full spoon to her lips, tips her head down, peers left and right, then lowers it to her bowl without taking in one little sip.

"Well, what the heck?" Dad says. "Everyone else is already at the bottom of their bowls."

He hurriedly walks to the pot and scoops a ladle and inhales the savory scent.

It all starts to happen at once. Behind me, I hear Dad cry, "No. Oh, no. No. No." Clooney yells, "What? What?" Someone in the dining room gags, followed by a retching noise. Then, from across the room, there's a disturbance, and Toddler Dad pushes back from his table and upchucks into his napkin.

Mom and I run into the dining room, waving our arms. "Don't eat any more soup!"

33

It's too late. Within ten minutes, the dining room is filled with the smell of sickness. Two people have puked all over themselves, and the other people at their table have clasped their hands over their noses to avoid the smell, including the two police officers.

Oops. There goes another one—it's one of the officers. The other officer joins him. All the sick people are at the same table. Maybe they got soup from the same pot. Hopefully, it's only one bad pot. Mom radios for backup and ambulances as the people around me swallow repeatedly and try not to blow chunks.

Two green-faced people are up and looking for extra napkins, and Billingsley is slowly making her way around them. She has her hand cupped over her nose as she moves toward the door.

Mom sees her officers are in distress, rushes over

to me, and says, "You get her bag—I'll get her." We take off after the dog-loving saboteur, who is just about out the door. I grab Billingsley's elbow and get a handful of sweater. It slows her down long enough for me to wrench her bag off her shoulder. Groucho pops his head out of it, barks, and leaps to the ground, and I lunge to catch him. Bag and dog in hand, I step back so Mom can get past me and follow Billingsley out the door.

Dad sees the chaos and yells, "Oh, no! My food!" He grabs two fistfuls of napkins and runs from table to table, handing them out. Mr. Lewis, who mentions that he's a doctor, offers to assist. Dad practically weeps as he says, "Thank you!"

Ben, who hadn't ordered any soup, runs to his uncle John, who is green and gagging but not throwing up. Ella, also not a soup eater, is trying to help the sisters. Dominic looks like he's in rough shape, but he's rushing to help his parents, who are also gasping for air. Mrs. Lewis is swallowing hard as her husband tends to her. Maybe not everyone got the bad soup, but we've all had our lunch ruined.

Zoe has her head down, her cheek flat against the table, and her mass of red hair halfway in the bowl. She's not barfing but she's green. The smell alone has turned other diners the same color.

I hurry outside to see if Mom needs any help. But Billingsley's on her belly, and Mom is already hand-cuffing her. Hubert nearly pushes me over when he comes barreling through the main door.

"What are you doing?" he yells. "Stop it! Hey! That's my mother!"

Mom orders him to stand back.

"Hubert," Billingsley shouts, "do something, you useless idiot!"

Sirens roar in the distance, and a Rook River squad car squeals onto the scene. Mom lets the uniformed officers get Billingsley up and read her the arrest rights. As an officer guides her into the squad car's back seat, Billingsley yells, "My dog. I want my dog!"

"Give me the dog," Hubert says.

"Not now," Mom replies. "We'll take it into protective custody and address that tomorrow."

I hand Mom the big purse, Groucho included. She puts it in the front seat of her squad car.

"This is illegal search and seizure," screams Billingsley.

"Pipe down," Mom says.

Then she turns to Hubert and tells him, "Meet me at my office in ten minutes and bring Willy. We're going to the station in Rook River."

As Billingsley kicks the Rook River squad car's protective steel mesh and bulletproof glass divider, one officer turns to another and says, "I think we're going to need some help on the other end."

Three ambulances from the fire and rescue station wail into town and turn into the parking lot, followed by another two police cars from Rook River.

The paramedics and extra officers flood into the café to help sick people and collect evidence, including the vomit samples, the pots of soup, and anything Billingsley touched. They have white paper masks on, but that doesn't keep three of them from gagging.

Mom says to one of the paramedics directing people into ambulances, "Can you handle all of this?"

He replies, "Yes, ma'am. It's what we do. But you better call the state health department. They're going to want to examine the food that did this."

She nods. "We have plenty of samples for them."

Thankfully, I'm told to stay outside with Groucho while they finish up.

Dad comes out of the restaurant and looks around for Mom. "I can't believe this. This is crazy. They're sick. From my cooking. Not in my lifetime. Not in generations. I feel terrible."

"I'm pretty sure Mrs. Billingsley poisoned the soup," I tell him.

"How? When?"

"I think it was when she went in the kitchen to wash the hot sauce bottle."

"You mean it *wasn't* my food?" Dad looks so relieved, I think he's going to cry.

Mom puts her arm around his waist. "No, honey. Not any ingredient you added."

* * *

Mom drives me, Groucho, and the big handbag back to her office at home. Because we're taking her squad car, I have to ride in the back like a perp. Groucho thinks it's fun, bouncing around and jumping at the chain mesh divider. I guess he and I are friends again.

Once we've arrived, Mom puts plastic down across the surface of her sheriff's desk and places the bag on top of it. She works her hands into surgical gloves and tags the bag as evidence. Then she starts examining the contents.

"It smells really bad," I say.

"The whole town smells bad," she says.

First, she pulls out a leather wallet with wet spots on it, then lipstick with the cap off, a lipstick cap, a pen, some receipts, a brush, and the incriminating evidence—two large plastic zip bags with the remnants of rotten fish in their corners.

She opens one of the bags, puts her nose near it, and reels back in revulsion. "I guess we know what went into the soup."

As she carefully re-zips the bag, there's a banging at the front of the house, and we both turn our heads.

Mom goes to the door, and I hear Hubert's voice. "What do I need to do to get my mother?"

"I see you didn't eat the soup," Mom says.

"No," he answers. "I don't eat fish myself. I'm allergic to it."

Mom looks at him skeptically. "Look, Hubert— she's involved in this. And I'm going to find out who else is. Where's Willy?"

"He's in the car."

"Then both of you get in the back of mine. I'm driving."

34

That night everyone—everyone who didn't order or managed not to eat the tainted fish soup—is gathered in the kitchen at the Boyd house. Ella, Ben, Mom, Dad, Clooney, and I are fine. Dominic and his parents, Zoe and her parents, Ms. Stillford, and Owen Loney are still at their homes, nursing their stomachs or recovering from secondhand queasiness. Beverly Billingsley is in jail. And so is the county health inspector. After interviewing Hubert and Willy, Mom learned that the inspector had been unsuccessfully trying to get money out of Hubert, the same way he had tried with Dad. He may not be on the hook for the soup, but he's under arrest for attempted extortion.

Mom is making coffee. Dad is baking brownies, even after I've tried to hint that people won't be hungry. I'd have Groucho on my lap to comfort me, but Mom turned him over to Hubert.

"What happens now?" Ben asks.

"I have to hire a toxicity abatement company to clean and treat the café," Dad says.

"That inspector," Mom says. "We found out he's been 'selling' passing inspections all over the county for about six months."

"What about Hubert?" I ask. "Any sign he knew about the Gusty's stuff?"

"Doesn't look like it," Mom says. "He and his mother have a very testy relationship. She's the one who pushed him to buy the lobster pound. He wanted to run an organic restaurant on a farm. She wanted him to be a Food Network star." Mom clasps her hands on the table. "He's horrified and wants to do whatever is necessary to compensate people."

"What about Willy?" Ben asks. "Did he pay off the inspector?"

"I asked him about what you boys saw. About the envelope." She laughs. "It was a payoff, but not for passing an inspection. Willy was giving the inspector a copy of Hubert's secret recipe for a Peruvian drink made with pineapple rinds in exchange for some cash. So, he might not be employed at Restaurant Hubert much longer, but he's not going to see any jail time."

"I can't believe Hubert didn't know about any of it," I say.

"Billingsley's admitted it, Quinnie," Mom says and pats my hand. "She wanted him to be a brand. She said she was frustrated with his lack of initiative. When he became a chef, she hoped he'd become big and famous in Boston, but he blew it. So when he came to Maiden Rock, she decided to watch over him. And when it looked like he might lose the contest, she thought if someone got sick at Gusty's, that would seal the deal."

"You mean she really was the man in black?" Ben asks with more than a little disbelief.

"Yes. She was the man in black."

"Wow," Ben says. "She's fast."

* * *

Before bed that night, Dad's sitting in the desk chair of my room. Mom's on the floor, leaning against the wall with her arms on her bent knees. Somehow she manages to make this look official. I'm on the bed, hugging my pillow.

No one is saying anything, and I haven't perfected the ability to keep my mouth shut in this kind of situation. "I should've stopped her before she got to the soup."

Mom says, "Maybe I should've picked up on

something when she asked me not to tell anyone she was Hubert's mother. But our guests make funny requests all the time."

"Where did she learn how to pick locks?" I ask.

"I don't know yet, but I'm sure we'll find that out too," Mom says.

"Do you think we'll get sued? Even though it wasn't our fault? Even though we were sabotaged?"

"I've already offered to pay people's medical bills." Dad's voice is so defeated.

"Won't Billingsley have to pay all that?" I feel a choke in my throat.

"Eventually, but it could take a while getting that through the courts," Mom says.

"I should've caught her so much earlier. It feels so rotten to fail." I feel the tears coming.

"No one failed, Quinnie." Mom sits forward. "It's complicated. Life's complicated. She got past us, by a critical few seconds. But she didn't get away. Thank goodness no one was seriously hurt. And I don't think the café's reputation will suffer long-term."

"I understand—it's complicated." I stop at that. I sure don't need my contributions to the complications examined in detail.

* * *

The *Rook River Valley Advertiser* covers the story extensively, and everyone in Maiden Rock learns what happened, who did it, how she did it, and who her son is. The paper states that authorities have not implicated Hubert Pivot in the crime and that three days after the contest's infamous final lunch, the health department has declared Gusty's safe for reopening.

The paper's Secret Diner has also waited to announce the winner of the competition until Gusty's started back up. Today's the day. The aroma of cinnamon buns, blueberry muffins, and espresso fills the café to its farthest corners. Many of our Maiden Rock neighbors and friends are here, waiting for Mom to bring the papers from the post office, where the Rook River paper delivery truck drops them off.

When Mom hurries in with a bundle of papers under her arm, a hush comes over the dining room. Dad grabs the stack from her and starts paging through the paper, looking for the column.

"Here it is!"

I feel so sorry for him. He's smiling, but the tips of the paper are shaking.

He starts to read. "'This critic compared the two restaurants in the coastal village of Maiden Rock over a two-week period, using my own unique criteria. Mwah hah hah! So let the critique begin.'"

Dad laughs nervously, and we all join him. "Funny guy, huh?" He clears his throat. "'Restaurant Hubert hit the local Maiden Rock food scene earlier this year, offering cutting edge culinary adventurousness of the highest quality, with small portions and hefty prices. It benefits from Chef Hubert Pivot's skill and inventiveness and the supreme atmosphere of Maiden Rock. It will be hard to forget the comically dramatic impact of the souffléed lobster quenelle.'"

There's a smattering of laughter around the room, but mostly tension fills the air.

Dominic leans over to me and says, "I think he's saving the winner to last."

I can't say anything because my throat is dry. I just dig my fingertips into his hand.

Dad clears his voice and continues. "'Gusty's Café has sat prominently on the side of the Maiden Rock Tidal Pool for generations, serving up authentic regional dishes and serving as a mainstay for locals and summer folk alike. Run by Gustav Boyd, the most recent in a line of Boyd family owners, the café maintains a comfort-food-based menu and a cozy atmosphere achieved through a certain amount of nurtured neglect. But we all know that old is not necessarily good. Sometimes it's just what's available.'"

Dad pauses. He looks like he's going to cry. Every face in the room is stricken.

Mr. Philpotts calls out, "Gus, keep reading!"

Dad raises the paper again like he's being led to an execution. "'However, that's not the case with Gusty's.'"

We all breathe a sigh of relief.

"'This café has consistently served some of the area's most reliable and delicious standards. To name a few items: Gusty burgers and lobster fries, a killer lobster roll, more-than-respectable clam chowder, cinnamon buns, whoopie pies, blueberry muffins and blueberry pie with real Maine blueberries, and a crab-cake-and-egg breakfast sandwich. Plus, he makes a mind-crushing double espresso.'"

Dad takes a breath, and the café erupts in applause and hoots. "Wait, wait. There's more." He reads on: "'Yet I would be shirking my solemn duty as a critic if I did not address the saga of the fish head soup.'"

Dad cringes, but there's no avoiding it. "'The people of coastal Maine have been eating fish head soup for as long as they've been fishing. It's good. It's hearty. Gusty's has been serving it off-menu forever. Why off-menu? Because most flatlanders can't abide the fish heads ogling at them from the bowl. But for this little competition, Gusty Boyd went public with the dish, modernized it nicely from a taste standpoint, and anointed it with kale and sea spray in a parody of Restaurant Hubert's gastro-decadence. I found it enchanting. And although the dish became the platform for an act of sabotage, Gusty Boyd is not to blame. Therefore, I declare Gusty's Café the winner of the Maiden Rock Secret Diner Competition.'"

After a rousing round of applause, people start pumping Dad's hand and slapping him on the back. I wait my turn since I know I'll get to squeeze the life out of him when the crowd backs off. When the café settles into breakfast, he walks over to our table.

"You and Dominic were right on with the fish head soup," he says.

"You made it happen. It's wonderful, Dad."

I hear murmuring ripple through the café. Hubert Pivot has walked through the door with a paper under his arm. Dad stiffens a little bit, but Hubert walks right up to him with his hand out for a shake.

"Gus. Congratulations."

"Thank you, Hubert."

"And another thing. I'd like to cover any of your expenses over the fish soup thing, so you don't have to wait for insurance payments or lawsuits or any-thing. Just send the claims my way."

Dad's eyebrows wrinkle like he's trying to under-stand what he just heard. "Really?"

"Yep. Really. She's my mother. I'll deal with it."

"Well, thank you, Hubert. Thanks very much."

Next, Hubert turns and walks over to the coun-ter. This part surprises me even more: he asks Owen Loney if Loney wants to buy back the lobster pound. "I can't see how I can do business in this town and not feel ashamed every day," he says.

Owen Loney proves himself to be a big man. "People around here wouldn't hold you responsible for a wayward relative. Though I don't think they're much for beams of light on their food."

"Maybe so, but it's not what I wanted anyway. I want to run a farm."

I hear a lightness in Owen Loney's voice that I've never heard before. "It would need to be turned back into a lobster pound. If I was to take it back, you know."

"How about you give me what I paid for it, plus, I'll turn it back to a pound?" Hubert offers. "It'll be exquisite. Like none other on the coast."

Owen Loney barely moves a muscle when he says, "Ayuh. You got yourself a deal."

35

What happened? I'm organizing stakeouts, creating spreadsheets, finding keys, and generally managing to not think about how Dominic's leaving, but suddenly there's a moving trailer in front of his house. From my bedroom window, I watch Dominic's mom and dad grunt and hoist boxes into their rented trailer. This is it. Soon their home of the last year will go back to being Zoe's house.

My feet feel like lead as I drag them next door, past the trailer, and up the stairs. I had promised myself I'd enjoy every minute of these last days, and then toxic fish head soup swallowed them up.

Pictures have come off the walls in the upstairs hallway. Only the hooks are left. I touch one and try to remember what photo had hung there, who was in the picture. Nope. Nothing. Dominic's family is fading from the house already.

I catch sight of Dominic's elbow on the other side of the doorframe. It's a denim-shirted elbow. I'm going to miss that denim-shirted elbow.

"Hey!" He's entirely too happy for this mournful day.

His room is nearly bare. The mattress is stripped of sheet and blankets. There are no Funko Pops in sight.

I perch myself on the sill of the ocean-side window. Buster and his seagull gang fly a figure eight over the beach, then dive for sand crabs. "You're going to text me, right?"

"I will text you and write you by snail mail and scare you with my geeky mug on Skype."

I want him to come over and stand by me, but he's finishing up taping the last box. "That'll be good," I say.

"I'm sure I'll see you soon," he says casually, but casual like people act when they're leaving somewhere they never intend to come back to.

"Right."

This is the moment when I'm ready for the big good-bye kiss. I wanted it, and then I didn't, and now I do. But he picks up his stuffed duffel bag and reaches for my hand. I give it to him, and he leads me down the stairs.

"I'm not going to the moon," he says, "just New Jersey."

So he's not going to miss me as much as I'm going to miss him. I get it. It makes me kind of sad-mad. But I get it.

Outside, Dominic's parents are packing in the last few things. I notice a pickup approaching the intersection and recognize it as John Denby's. He turns the corner and pulls up behind the moving trailer. Ben's in the passenger seat with his head out the window. "Ready to go?" he calls out to Dominic.

Dominic, still carrying the duffel bag, walks over to the pickup and slings it in the box. Then he gives his mom and dad a big hug.

"What's going on?" I ask.

"Oh, wait. Didn't I tell you? I'm spending the rest of the summer at Ben's."

I feel like I just washed my face with a warm washcloth on a winter day. So good. So happy.

Dominic throws his arm around my shoulder for a big squeeze. For the first full, wide-open moment of summer, I am carefree.

"Hey!" Ella's voice calls to me from the direction of her house. She and Zoe dash up together, one in silver-sparkle tennis shoes, the other with bouncing red locks. "We came to say good-bye."

"He's not leaving yet," I say. I know I have a stupid grin on my face. "He's staying with Ben for the rest of the summer."

Ella gives Ben's arm a punch. "You didn't tell me!"

He pretends to flinch. "Ouch! It was a surprise. It's like your dad's detective, Monroe Spalding, says: 'It's the thing you don't think of that's most significant.'"

"Aw," she says. "How sweet. You've been reading my dad's books."

"Not exactly," Ben replies. "There's a popular quotes section on the Monroe Spalding Wikipedia page."

Ella leans her head on Ben's arm, and Dominic takes my hand and locks fingers with me. It feels *most significant*.

Acknowledgments

Thanks to my entire family, and especially to Chuck Hanebuth and Magda Surrisi, who support me in every possible way, and to Ellie and Michael, who are eagerly awaiting this book. To the entire VCFA tribe, and to the Magic Ifs and Magic Sevens, the SCBWI gang, the Asheville Secret Gardeners, and my other writing friends everywhere—you know who you are.

To our family of friends in Asheville who have become so dear, especially Anne Wall and Reina Weiner, who have been beta readers for me. And to Will Hart, my middle-grade beta reader for the three Quinnie Boyd Mysteries, who is without question Quinnie's biggest fan, and who said of this one, "I couldn't believe who did it!" There's nothing a mystery writer likes more than that!

Thanks to all the great people at Lerner, who make beautiful books, and especially one of the smartest people I know, my editor Greg Hunter, who exemplifies excellence and is a gracious guiding hand—and truly, special thanks to him for loving Quinnie Boyd as much as I do. And to Linda Pratt, who is not only my agent but a lifelong friend. She always finds the time to talk and read and give great feedback. Finally, to Julie McLaughlin, for creating the most delicious cover for this volume.

About the Author

C. M. Surrisi lives in Asheville, North Carolina, with her husband Chuck and two rascal Cavalier King Charles Spaniels named Sunny and Milo. She is a graduate of the Vermont College of Fine Arts MFA program in Writing for Children and Young Adults.